hotel crystal

Originally published in French as *Suite à l'hôtel Crystal*
by Éditions du Seuil, 2004

Copyright © Éditions du Seuil, 2004
Collection La Librairie du XXIe siècle, sous la direction de Maurice Olender
Translation copyright © 2008 by Jane Kuntz

First English translation, 2008

Library of Congress Cataloging-in-Publication Data

Rolin, Olivier.
[Suite à l'hôtel Crystal. English]
Hotel crystal / Olivier Rolin ; translation by Jane Kuntz.
p. cm.
Includes index.
ISBN-13: 978-1-56478-492-6 (alk. paper)
ISBN-10: 1-56478-492-4 (alk. paper)
I. Kuntz, Jane. II. Title.
PQ2678.O4155S8513 2008
843'.914--dc22
2007043740

Partially funded by a grant from the Illinois Arts Council, a state agency,
and by the University of Illinois at Urbana-Champaign

This work has been published, in part, thanks to the
French Ministry of Culture – National Book Center

www.dalkeyarchive.com

Cover art by Nicholas Motte
Design by Danielle Dutton
Printed on permanent/durable acid-free paper
and bound in the United States of America

hotel crystal
olivier rolin

Translated from the French by Jane Kuntz
Dalkey Archive Press ▣ Champaign and London

"Were each man not able to live a number of lives other than his, he would be unable to live his own."
Paul Valéry, *Variété*

"I have an exceptional—I believe fairly prodigious even— memory of all the places I have slept in."
Georges Perec, *Species of Spaces*

Contents

Forward

Let us review the facts. Some six months after the disappearance[1] of the author of these texts—collected here for the first time in a systematic and critical fashion—Madame ***, one of the author's close acquaintances, having lost her briefcase somewhere on the way between her home and her office, tries her luck at the lost-and-found department located on Rue des Morillons in the 15th arrondissement of Paris. She finds no trace of it there, but she does recognize, unmistakable amidst a disparate assortment of other items, the expandable accordion briefcase belonging to her missing friend, with whom she had traveled on numerous occasions. The briefcase in question was left behind in a taxi, and it had proven impossible to trace it back to its "loser"—which is what the clerks at the Rue des Morillons call the absentminded. The time having elapsed without anyone coming to claim the item, they relinquished it to her. Once opened, it turned out to contain—apart from a few articles of clothing—a small pile of books and papers (21 x 29.7 centimeters handwritten sheets, printed documents, pages removed from small or large notebooks, endpapers ripped out of bound books, envelopes, hotel stationary, postcards, the backs of maps, etc.). Despite these disparate formats,[2] the texts themselves have this much in com-

---

1   Under well-known circumstances (see "room" 20, note 2, and "room" 22).
2   We have listed the paper format in a note following each text.

mon: each describes a hotel room in minute detail—something like a detective at a crime scene might—then goes on to relate an anecdote involving the author and this particular location.

What exactly would the structure of this unfinished book have been, whose individual "rooms" could be seen as scattered bricks, not yet assembled? Was such a project even planned? These are things that we will never know for certain. We are reasonably sure, nevertheless, that the second question can be answered in the affirmative. Otherwise, it would be difficult to explain the author's sustained, systematic effort, writing his "topautobiographical" notes. (We hope the reader will forgive this neologism whereby we attempt to explain the relationship— quite rare in the history of literature, and to be honest, somewhat incongruous—between a "state of settings or places" (*topos*) and a fragmented, incomplete autobiographical narrative). That a project existed seems highly likely. What could it have been? We are reduced to mere conjecture. The author does, in fact, seem to provide answers to this query,[3] but there is no way to be certain that this isn't a trap set to mislead us. Doomed as we are to ignorance of intentions, the only thing we feel we can reasonably surmise is that the texts contained in the briefcase were to be read, as it were, in light of the pair of quotations— one from Paul Valéry, the other from Georges Perec—which he scribbled on the back of a Tokyo-Hiroshima train ticket dated June 15, 2003, and which for this reason we decided to include

---

3   See "room" 20, note 2 of that section, p. 95, where we discuss this question. See also the examination of a clever hypothesis in "room" 37, note 1.

as our epigraph. It is a modest and plausible assumption, albeit far from definitive.

We could find no explicit indications that would enable us to establish an order among the loose texts. The one posited here is therefore entirely of our own design. Various things in the text (relationships among characters, etc.) suggested it to us; yet it still allows certain oddities, inconsistencies, and contradictions to persist, as undoubtedly they must in any unfinished project. Be that as it may, several other ordering systems might well be possible (perhaps even an infinite number). Needless to say, the index is also our work. In addition, we included as author's notes (AN) bits of text that, for the most part, do not figure in the manuscript (or, rather, manuscripts) proper, but appear in the margins, or in another color ink, between the lines, and as such seemed not so much a development of the text as a commentary thereupon. The text we put at the end of this book (43[4]) can be interpreted in a number of ways: one could think of it as a kind of prose poem inspired by (or modeled upon) Cendrars or Larbaud. Alternatively—and we favor this hypothesis—it might simply act as a set of notes made with the intention of writing further "rooms." In either case, it seemed like the proper conclusion to this collection.

Finally, we feel it is our duty to mention that the rather implausible circumstances under which these papers were recovered have caused some people to suspect a hoax. Indeed, it should be acknowledged that several texts (notably 39) may well

---

4   The title, "The Full Stop Hotel," is ours.

lend credence to that suspicion, seeming to function like the clues some ironic counterfeiter might imbed in his work. Still, there are numerous considerations—stylistic, graphological, biographical, and even psychological—that persuade us to reject this hypothesis as exaggeratedly complicated and even a bit paranoid.[5] If we might add a wholly personal consideration—one that owes nothing to critical analysis and everything to the romantic view we have of the world—we would say that, far from being a mark of intrigue, the very strangeness of the conditions under which these pages came into our hands is the seal of their authenticity. *Mirum verum:* the real is wondrous.

The Editors

---

5   To take just one example, a biographical one: it turns out that the author did in fact travel by the Shinkansen train from Tokyo to Hiroshima on the 15th of June 2003. Can you imagine the level of organization that would be required to disguise the false beneath the true, not once or twice but multiple times? Readers who want to know more should refer to the very thorough study on the subject in the *Journal of Pseudology,* number 22.

1

Room 308, Заполарье Гостиница (The Polar Hotel), Khatanga:

The room measures about 4 x 5 meters. A partition with a 2.5 x 1 meters opening in the middle divides it into two parts (in the manner of an iconostasis): a narrow entryway about one meter wide along the entire width of the room; then, behind the partition, the room itself. The door is painted white, the hall khaki, and the frame of the entryway to the room forms a white arch. Brown baseboards run along the walls. The floor is covered in a (poor) imitation parquet linoleum. The ceiling, about 3 meters high, is painted white. To the right of the entrance, a small blue apparatus labeled "50 лет Поъеды" (50th Anniversary of the Victory), purpose unknown, is affixed to the wall, level with the top of the door. Below are two switches. The wall to the left of the entrance features a white ceramic sink with a large oval mirror, into which—upon coming in from outdoors—I laugh at my face, scorched by the cold beneath my wolf-skin *chapka*. To the right, the narrow, metallic double doors of the wardrobe. From the ceiling hangs a bare light bulb.

The walls of the room itself are papered in vertical strips with a brown floral motif against a grayish-beige background imitating a fabric weave. Two single beds covered with a kind of tarpaulin decorated with yellow and brown flowers sit on opposite sides of the room. Between the "iconostasis" partition and the foot of each of the beds is a rather rickety wooden chair. A window is set into the wall facing the entrance, about 1.75 x 1.75 meters square, twin casement and double paned. The panes are stuck closed, and only a small transom above to the right opens. The outside panes are covered on their inner sides (if you are following this) with a crust of ice. Beneath the window is an enormous cast-iron radiator, in front of which sits a square, pale green Formica-topped table covered with an oilskin tablecloth: brown flowers on a white background. On the ceiling, the light fixture looks exactly like a frosted, upside-down cognac glass.

I knocked back a few dozen of glasses of cognac—that is, the rotgut syrup that goes by that name in Russia—with Gricha at the Aviation Bar, a simple little joint on the ground floor of the hotel with deep red plush walls and a television set. Sitting on a shelf, somewhat incongruously, is a fan. A limp, languid blonde serves as bartender (among other things). Gricha is Colonel Grygor Ilyuchinsk, former armored tank division boxing champion, whence his broken nose, as well as his missing right ear, torn off by a bullet in Afghanistan; Gricha, one hundred kilos of meat, whose rare smile, as in Baudelaire's "Dancing Serpent," mixes "gold with iron," whose sandpaper skull is shielded from the cold by a red wool cap, who's forever dressed in army fatigues and an aviator jacket, the biggest cognac drinker I've ever known, a pure heart. He's used to making a living pimping a few girls, including Severina, the fat blonde at the Aviator, and by exploiting a gang of lowlife thugs who fish and hunt for him on the tundra. At the wheel of his ГАЗ truck, he goes every month to pick up reindeer hides or blue fox pelts, stiff as sheet metal, or ingots of frozen salmon, in exchange for a few bottles of vodka and the occasional fist in the face.

Perched atop the red-hot radiator, standing on tiptoe (like a guy clumsily trying to hang himself in a hotel room in Buenos Aires—like Sergeï Antonomarenko, but that's another story, which I'll tell in good time), I opened the transom above and to the right of the inner window of room 308, and scraped the ice out from between the two panes. Each time I exhale, my breath deposits a light film of ice on the glass, which I then have to brush away, my hand acting as a windshield wiper. Through this newly improvised view, I see the shiny sheet-metal roof of the airport to the right, a four-engine Antonov on the tarmac, a few buildings made of brick or sheet-metal, long sheds with wooden or sheet metal roofs, brown or lime-colored, a fuel tank, tall, spindly smokestacks, wired, plumed with smoke, wooden electrical poles, a battered, oil-encrusted tanker truck. A few figures, bundled up and wearing felt boots, waddle across the dirty snow. In the midst of all this, I focus especially on Gricha proceeding to load the Antonov: huge, gesticulating, yelling (I can't hear him, of course, but I see his face tense up rhythmically. Gricha has what one might call an unexpressive face. By that I mean that certain expressions, anger or defiance for example, show up better on his than on others.). The nuclear warheads are set on six tarpaulin-covered trailers pulled by two tractors.

Some well-preserved ordnance, never used—forgotten since the collapse of the USSR in the underground installations at Khatanga. At the Aviation Bar, tongue loosened by liquor, Gricha told me he was looking for a client. I call Crook, a former MI6 man fired for compulsive lying and drug abuse—an artist, a virtuoso when it comes to shady deals and dirty tricks. Crook knows the whole world—that is, the upper tiers of the international cutthroat set. It didn't take him more than a couple of days to put us in touch with the Beloved Leader of the Rpop#%µ©!!¾œ☐2&.[1] I think I had a lot to do with the success of this transaction. Ilyuchinsk's small-time connections couldn't have helped him palm off the goods. And yet, something tells me he's trying to give me the slip. Someone, actually: Severina. Her gossip can't always be trusted—she's not exactly bright, after all, and the poor girl thinks she's going to escape with me from Khatanga, this Siberian pit, north of the Arctic Circle. Still . . . I'm uneasy. That's why I'm perched awkwardly on the radiator of room 308, secretly checking things out through a hole scraped into the ice on the outside pane of my window. It's crazy: what could I possibly find out like this? But I can't help it. A group of drunks can be heard bellowing in the hallway. Doors slam violently.

Text handwritten on three pages torn out of Victor Hugo's Les Misérables, *published by Laffont in the Bouquins Collection.*

---

1   Decode as you will. For more on this, see the "room" 34, note 2. *(EN)*

2

Room 1210, Norals Beach Hotel, Tahr-el-Bahr Street, Port Saïd:

It's a very complicated room to describe. Very long, perhaps a dozen meters, more like a small apartment. What you have to understand is that the wall to your right as you enter runs in a straight, unadorned line all the way to the balcony (if you don't count the pilaster-style pillar that stands out a few centimeters facing the bathroom), while on the left, the surfaces vary, inset at different depths. There's nothing along this right-hand wall except, near the beds, a small table with two drawers and a mirror hung above it (where, for once, I see a reflection of myself that doesn't offend me: tan, slim, clean-shaven, a licentious look in my eyes), and above that, a light.

First, the front door, made of roughly varnished wood (daubed with dark splotches), opens onto an antechamber of about 3 x 3 meters where, on the left, beneath a frosted glass transom framed in royal blue, sits a low yellowish wooden table flanked by two chairs made out of the same wood, painted in a greenish-yellow—probably military issue—and upholstered in a mottled yellow fabric. Past which is the bathroom, whose door is brownish wood in a white frame about one meter wide. Mottled brown and beige carpet, the same throughout the room. Walls and ceiling painted white.

The bedroom proper measures about 6 x 4 meters. To the right, as stated earlier, the table-mirror-light cluster. Against the left-hand wall sits a little Gorenje-brand fridge, hopelessly out of order, set in a wooden cabinet painted greenish-yellow, followed by two yellowish wooden closet doors. The twin beds are set perpendicular to the wall facing the mirror. The bedspreads are a sea-green diamond pattern, cotton fabric, printed with pale yellow shapes vaguely resembling stars. The headboards—the same for both beds—are painted yellowish-green, or brownish, or dirty chartreuse, whatever, with a padding covered in the same yellowish mottled fabric as the chairs in the antechamber. To the right or left of each bed, a black lamp on a night table with a drawer. There's a telephone on left-hand table, one with an old-fashioned dial: pea green, with so-called "Arabic" numerals, which is to say, Indian, ours, 1, 2, 3, 4, 5, etc., as well as Arab numbers, ١, ٢, ٣, ٤, ٥, etc.

The back wall, facing the entrance, is broken up by a two-foot tall sliding door composed of two pieces of plate glass set in an aluminum frame painted royal blue.

The draperies are cut from the same cloth as the bedspreads. The sliding door opens onto a balcony, about 2 x 4 meters, with tile flooring (tiling on the floor?) in a black and gray floral pattern, closed off by a metal railing that's peeling royal blue. There are two chairs and a rattan table bearing an ancient coat of white paint (it should be pointed out—and I pointed it out to Leila—that these chairs are exactly the same kind as the ones in the apartment where I lived as a child with my parents, on Avenue C . . . in Dakar (Senegal): a kind of flared black metal netting, called "Knoll," I believe). Just beyond, a tree with large, shiny leaves, maybe a rubber tree, though I can't be certain. Lawns and lanes lined with miniature palm trees, at the end of which an empty swimming pool of some indefinable shape, let's say rounded, fitted with mauve tiles, and another hotel building can be seen. Streetlamps, parasols. And then the beach, looking rather like a dump, the waves, the blurry clouds, the fishing boats trawling just offshore, cargo ships anchored or slowly approaching the canal entrance, to the right.

How many nights did I spend on that balcony in Leila's bewitching company, drinking gin-and-tonics overlooking the sea where Themistocles Papadiamntides's dhow was supposed to appear—henceforward our only hope of salvation? Leila, third daughter of the third wife of the imam of the Al Azhar mosque, whom I snatched away right from under her father's nose. She caught my eye at an embassy where I have privileged access, and where she was working as a secretary. She had a hoarse voice and parasol eyelashes, she spoke English with rolled *r*s and smoked filtered Egyptian cigarettes whose smoke made her eyes water; she also had a remarkable beauty mark on her right breast, but that, of course, wasn't something I noticed right away. I invited her to dine at a floating restaurant on the Nile the same evening we met, and it wasn't long, then, before the beauty mark was discovered. Given her father's profession, we were soon being chased around by half the fanatics in the Middle East (where they're legion). I managed to contact Papadiamantides, whom I'd done a favor for a few years earlier in the business of the sham shipwreck of the *Monika,* and he agreed to smuggle us out, which is why we were there waiting for him, Leila and I, drinking gin-and-tonics all day and screwing copiously all night (or the other way around), in room 1210 of the Norals Beach Hotel, Tahr-el-Bahr Street, in Port Saïd. All told, this room, despite the somewhat unfortunate choice of colors, was surprisingly pleasant.

Text handwritten on graph paper torn out of a schoolboy's notebook.

3

Room 226, Torni Hotel, Yrjönkatu 26, Helsinki:

Another room more complicated to describe than the average. The door opens into a little entryway of around 2.5 x 2.5 meters, onto which opens, on the right, after the mirror, the door to the bathroom, and, on the left, a closet made of blond wood (birch, perhaps? Anyway, all the other furniture in this room—I'm pointing this out now so that I don't have to come back to it—is made out of the same wood.). The ceiling, about 2.5 meters high, features a frosted glass porthole right in its center, currently illuminated. To the right of the door on entering, a thermometer that currently reads 22°C.

The main room, cubic like the entrance but more spacious, must measure approximately 4.5 x 4.5 x 4.5 meters: a high ceiling, therefore, with a large rhomboidal brass crown at its center (I'm not sure if I'm making myself clear), fitted tightly around a polished glass fixture—another light. The carpet is green, flecked with a little red and yellow motif of nondescript shape. On the right-hand wall, a large mirror sits atop a table with two drawers, plain and functional. Up against this table sits a two-tiered chest, each tier closed by a two-panel articulated wooden door, containing a minibar below and a Nokia television set above. Facing the door, a double-paned window, relatively narrow (about 1.50 x 2.50 meters), looks out onto a small paved courtyard where, under a lime tree that the wind has now stripped of its leaves, sits a pile of stacked chairs and tables, remnants of the summer season, as well as space heaters for the bistro terrace. Above, a modern building where shining neon letters spell out TEKNISKA FÖRENINGEN I FINLAND, evidently in Swedish, since I can almost make out the meaning. Triple curtains shield the windows: white cloth, then white netting, then pale beige velvet. Beneath is a flat radiator.

To the left of the window, the wall is hung like all the others with wallpaper in broad stripes of very pale beige and bister, topped with the image of a strip of green acanthus leaves twirled around a fascia, about 50 centimeters from the ceiling. The upper part of the walls is white, as is the ceiling. Abutting this same wall is a single bed covered with a bedspread in a green leaf print on white background, whose rather tall headboard faces the window, and above which is hung a small painting by a certain Kohlmann, depicting a bridge over a stream set in a snowy landscape with a pine forest in the background. On the night table—the same wood and simple design as the rest of the furniture—is a lamp composed of a flattened globe of frosted glass (jellyfish-like) held in place by a brass ring attached by three curved arms to a fluted brass column set in the center of a brass disk (the lamp sits on the table just beneath the mirror). A high-backed chair and an armchair tending toward the ellipsoidal (or something)—upholstered in a blazing pink with white dotted lines running through it—complete the furniture.

It's in the mirror above the table, with fewer than a hundred days remaining until the end of the twentieth century, that I stare at my face, busted up, oozing, bruised and bandaged, squeezed into a kind of girdle of netting, in sharply painful (and sarcastic) contrast with the photo, older and exaggeratedly glamorous, of the same individual (or, one might say, of another individual bearing the same name, having written a book in French entitled *Port-Soudan*), published in the *"Kulttuuri"* pages of the *Helsingin Sanomat,* dated *Sunnuntaina* 3, *Iokakuuta* 1999, lying open across the leather blotter on the table. A roll of gauze on the left side of my skull makes me look like a giant Mickey Mouse that had its other ear bitten off by a cat. In the postwar years, the Torni Hotel used to be the GPU headquarters in Helsinki, and I look just like I've come out of a heated discussion with the comrades (that's where Antonomarenko began his career, in the mid-fifties). In fact, three days ago, totally drunk, I got into a brawl over an interpretation of the Sibelius D Minor Violin Concerto with some sailors in a bar down by the port, and the disagreement failed to turn to my advantage. I was dragged to the Maria Hospital in the midst of a Shakespearian tempest. And, at present, I'm staring at my bumpy, blotchy face, packed into its netting, comparing it by lamplight to my skull-and-crossbones likeness in an x-ray image marked "Olivier Rolin, 05/17/57, 10/8/99, Forum," taken at the Forumin Lääkäriasema Mannerheimintie 20B, a private clinic near the hotel where I'm a regular. They made a ten-year error in my date of birth, from which I deduce (through a torturous kind of logic that nonetheless strikes me as quite obvious) that I am to live only ten more years before this last face becomes mine—a definitively generic Jolly Roger. See you in October 2009.

Text handwritten on a white envelope, 21 x 27 centimeters, stationary of the Forumin Lääkäriasema, Mannerheimintie 20B.

- 4 -

Room 514, Royal Savoy, Lausanne:

The entryway, papered in pink moiré, as is the rest of the room, offers a gold-framed mirror to the curious eye, and a luminous globe of streaked glass on the ceiling. In the lock is a key whose heavy brass ornament (a ball covered in rubber) seems to be in perpetual motion. To the right, a door opens into the bathroom.

To the left, upon entering the room, a classic engraving graces the pink wall above the baggage rack made of dark wooden slats: *Entering the Stable* (Paris, Jazet's, drawing by C. Vernet). Next, there's the no-less-classic black minibar and black television (Nokia), then a roll-top desk in oak, three drawers, topped with a standard issue hotel lamp, whose oval shade conceals two imitation candles, the whole thing made of brass (or bronze?), as usual.

On the opposite wall, a tall radiator is jammed right up against the desk. Double drapes, mingling pink, green, and beige, held in place with tiebacks, frame a window that opens onto a balcony and the lake. At night, when there is no mist, you can see the glittering orange lights of Evian on the opposite shore. When it's misty, the sooty nearby silhouette of what must be an enormous cypress tree conjures up images of the arctic mirages that illustrate my childhood copy of *Captain Hatteras*, the Hetzel edition.

The carpet is of palest blue flecked with white. An armchair, upholstered in the same pink/green/beige stripes as the drapes, sits beside a little round, four-legged table. The large double bed with its white bedspread is flanked by two night tables in pale oak, each bearing a brass lamp with a white shade. To the right of the door, an oak wardrobe is set against the wall facing the window. A crystal chandelier dangles from the white lacquer ceiling.

I'm lounging in my bath when the door to the room opens, making way for a chambermaid dressed (from what I could make out) in a white smock and black stockings. A black velvet bow holds her blond chignon in place, letting a few wisps of hair escape. The bathroom door is wide open. Astonished that she doesn't just run away, I start to make watery noises, tentative at first, then increasingly noisy. She doesn't pay the least attention and sets about her chore of making the bed. I emerge from the bathtub in a great splash; she seems oblivious. She removes the used bed linens, stuffs them into a canvas bag, goes out into the hall for a moment, brings back a pair of clean sheets, and begins to make the bed. I come out of the bathroom, stark naked, grab her from behind by the waist and push her onto the bed; she says nothing, doesn't move a muscle. I turn her over and start undressing her, which she lets me do, remaining motionless. I notice then that she's rather pretty, though her nose is a bit large, in my opinion—but her breasts are milky white. We fuck—or, it would be more accurate to say: I fuck her. It's over. She showed neither pleasure nor disgust, no emotion of any kind; she neither

groaned nor cried out, never said a word, didn't make the slightest movement. She gets back up, dresses, her mind elsewhere.
She removes the sheets she just put on the bed, stuffs them into
the canvas bag, and goes out into the hallway to get a new pair.
She spreads them out, tucks them in, lays out the bedspread,
patting it to smooth down the wrinkles. Not knowing what to
do with myself, I return to the bathroom and get back into the
tub. She follows me into the bathroom, changes the soaps and
towels. At one point, I wonder if she's going to unplug the drain,
empty the bath water, scrub down the tub and toss me out with
the dirty towels. But she doesn't, and is soon on her way.

Text handwritten in the margins of a concert program
(Jane Birkin, Arabesque, *Châtelet Theater, 2 March 2004).*

Room 18, Hostellerie de la Mer, Le Fret (Crozon):

One enters the room through a small, rectangular vestibule, about 1.5 x 1 meters, with walls hung in a plasticized, heavy weave, sack-like fabric, in brown/white/ochre stripes (uneven). The short-piled carpet is printed in a pattern of interlocking right angles and V-shapes. Facing the door, made of two-toned wood (red mahogany and brown oak, roughly), is another door, to the bathroom, similarly two-toned, and to the left, still another, of the same model, that opens into the main room. The number 23 is painted on it in white: probably a reused apartment.

The room proper measures about 4 x 7 meters. To the right of the door upon entering, set into the width of the rectangle, is a wardrobe with oak doors sculpted in geometrical patterns, swirling and pyramidal. It doesn't quite fill the recess: above it there's an empty space, concealed by a pink canvas apron, where the bed linens are stored. The walls are covered in a plasticized fabric with vertical stripes of sepia and rosy beige, as well as white braid. On the floor: a short-piled, anthracite-colored carpet. The oak bed frame, carved just like the wardrobe, is set perpendicular to the wall, with the headboard up against the wall to the right, and is covered with a spread made of the same dusty pink, rough woven fabric as the aforementioned apron. On either side, each of two oak wall mounts bear a small lamp consisting of a pink porcelain sphere topped by a white shade with pink braiding. To the right of the headboard are two straw-bottomed chairs. To the left, under the wall mount, an ivory-colored telephone sits on a small bedside table made of oak, carved with the same motifs as the wardrobe and the bed, and covered with a white doily.

Another bed, a small single made of stained bamboo, covered with a bedspread of the pink fabric mentioned earlier, is set beneath the window, which is painted white and divided into four rows of six little panes, taking up about 1.5 x 1.75 meters of the wall facing the door. From here one can see the freight dock, two lampposts, and a few small boats moored on the black water. Far-off lights too, and the orange nimbus of Brest. The faint sound of surf and the light clinking of the halyards produce a pleasing lullaby.

The long wall to the left of the entrance is bare, except for a little square-legged table, in oak, covered with a white cloth. Between this table and the window sits a large cast-iron radiator, painted white. The ceiling, also painted white, is relatively low, sloping toward the window. An odd chandelier hangs from it, composed of a wooden ring bearing two imitation candlesticks fitted with electric candles and connected by a kind of wooden yoke, suspended from a short chain. On the two lengthwise walls, both behind and facing the bed, hang two small portraits of Breton women in their headdresses, attributed to one Daniel Derveaux.

A pleasing lullaby is indeed what we needed, my old Master Louis Althusser and I, on the night we spent in room 18 of the

Hostellerie de la Mer. It was just a few years after the so-called "'68"[1] events. He got it into his head, as he would recall in his posthumous memoirs, to steal an atomic submarine. Through the bathroom transom, one could make out the nearby sodium lights at the Longue Isle base. Did this business seem straightforward to my old Master, in his delirium, or had he just decided on a rather complicated way to kill himself? Whatever the case, he had purchased an officer's uniform in dark blue wool at the Clichy flea market, on which—after referring to the *Larousse Encyclopedia of the Twentieth Century*—he sewed five gold stripes corresponding to the rank of ship's captain. With the face of a manic-depressive spaniel under his ornamental officer's cap, he would have been laughable, were it not for the nerve-racking circumstances, as he chain-smoked Gauloises that night, seated on the little bamboo bed beneath the window (he absolutely insisted that I sleep in the double). His plan consisted of simply showing up the next day at the entrance to the base and informing the maritime gendarmerie that he was the new commander of the *Redoutable,* appointed at a Council of Ministers that same morning (this detail struck him as tremendously cunning, likely to allay any suspicion). I, on the other hand, harbored grave doubts as to the reliability of this scheme, but I had too much respect for the philosopher who had helped me discover scientific Marxism not to go along with it. I just

---

1   Mistakenly so. I could demonstrate that the so-called "'68" events did not take place in '68. But that's another story, which I will tell another time, if I get around to it. *(AN)*

pointed out to my old Master that it was (probably) forbidden to smoke aboard a nuclear submarine. The proletariat is going to change all that, Rolin, he replied from inside a bluish cloud. All the same, I persisted, all the same: he shouldn't show up at the security check-point with a cigarette hanging from his mouth; it just wasn't very ship's captain-like, in my view. We'll see, we'll see, was his cagey reply. Then, putting out his Gauloise: All right, let's get some sleep. And soon that's what we were doing, rocked by the faint sound of surf, the light clinking of the halyards.

Text handwritten on the back of a "Tourist Map of the Crozon Peninsula."

6

Room 18, Vendegház Astra, Vám utca 6, Budapest:

The room is square, very large (about 6 x 6 meters), with walls and ceiling painted white. The floor is a herringbone parquet, a true rarity in hotel rooms (if memory serves, I've encountered only one other parquet-floored hotel room, in Coimbra, Portugal; but that's another story, which I'll tell when the time comes). I'm drinking some *körtepálinka*, Vilmos brand, 80 proof, dear God. The arched doorway is located near one of the angles of the room's square. Along the wall, to the right when you come in, there are, first, a sideboard in an orangey (carroty?) wood, upon which are a Samsung TV set and an oblong silver metal tray holding four glasses (two large cylindrical ones, and two small stemmed glasses, one of which I'm using to drink, dear God, this *pálinka*); then, on a stand made of the same wood, the Goldstar minibar—whence the *pálinka*, which costs 500 forints, as noted on the form; then a dresser of the same carroty wood (like all the other furniture), with four drawers one atop the other, surmounted finally by a square mirror in a wooden frame. I take a look at myself, absentmindedly: cropped hair, big snout, dark rings under the eyes, a two-day beard. White shirt, and a double-breasted black linen suit. A shady kind of stylishness.

I need to brace myself with this 500-forint *pálinka* because I've just—quite unexpectedly—committed a crime. Not that I'm one of those housebound writers frightened by the idea of murder, no. But normally one has the time to prepare for it psychologically, whereas, in this case . . . It happened like this: I was to rendezvous on Jozef-Attila Street with Pashmina Pachelbel, a former Miss Turkey, who was performing in an advanced state of undress at the Gellert Baths. The bright cyclops eye of Tram 39 made its way along the Danube, the Chain Bridge I was walking across glittered with a thousand lights, and when I turned around, the castle and all the churches of Buda were crisply etched against a moonlit sky of mauve velvet. I was feeling carefree. Suddenly, I heard the sound of a pair of crepe-soled shoes behind me. What's more, when I strained to listen, I seemed to recognize the signature sibilance of Antonomarenko's crepe soles in particular. What would happen next (if it was indeed him) was easy to predict: the piano wire drawing nimbly around my neck, my trachea crushed, my corpse sending up a spray of foam as it fell into the dark water of the Danube below. Thank you very much. Unsheathing the sharpened (and ricin-tipped) sword concealed in my umbrella, I spun around and ran it through the man in the crepe-soled shoes. Stabbed through the heart, he fell without a sound (though in a pool of blood). It wasn't Antonomarenko, as far as I could tell—it was some priest. I admit to having acted somewhat hastily, but with characters like Antonomarenko, survival often comes at such a price: it's them or you (actually, as far as Antonomarenko's concerned, he won't be bothering anyone anymore: it seems he's hanged himself in Buenos Aires). I briskly pushed the cleric over the parapet. His small stature made the job easier. All told, things could have been worse. No one had seen me. I could conceive (I conceived for a fraction of a second) of making my way peacefully to my rendezvous with Pashmina Pachelbel, with whom I would spend the rest of the evening as if nothing had happened. As luck would have it, however, at that precise instant, pushing the priest over, one of those pathetic little tourist boats they call U-Boats suddenly came out from under the bridge. Tourists were dining on the upper deck. The clergyman landed right in their soup. Dreadful crashing, hysterical screams. I left as though I hadn't noticed anything. Now I'm bracing myself with *körtepálinka* in room 18 of the Vendegház Astra, which contains nothing remarkable apart from the bed where I firmly intended to fuck Pashmina Pachelbel. Alas! It's one of those absolutely enormous king-size set-ups that can sleep six (a song from my childhood comes to mind, "In the middle of the riverbed, the water is deep / all the king's horses can drink there as one"). Each of the carrot-wood night tables on either side holds an imitation brass lamp with a three-footed base with a vaguely leafy motif and a frilly lampshade; the table to the left of the bed also sports a Matel telephone. But that bed! Head and foot made of curved wood like a bow ornament on a Greek galley, covered with a bedspread of beige velour, three pillows covered in the same fabric, each with a fancy trim that makes them look like gigantic ravioli. Above it all, set in a gilt frame, a painting in dusky tones, very Rembrandt-like, portraying a table upon which are books whose bindings shine dimly—one lying open displaying pages of feminine white—as well as a candlestick and an ashtray whose rounded glass gleams, cradling a lit cigarette. Not bad. Transtemporal.

In the third wall, entirely bare and white, is an archway that opens onto a little antechamber that leads into the bathroom. On either side hang two small engravings in dark wooden frames: *De Essekker Brugh,* taken from a series entitled *Civitates Hungariae Inferioris;* and one of two women, one standing in a large, black crinoline dress, reading a letter, the other seated, deporting herself modestly, as they say. One presumes (codes are codes) that the letter is from a lover (and that the more modest of the two is the confidante—but the seated position precludes her being a servant).

Cut out of the far wall, the one that meets back up with the doorway, and thus faces the bed, there's a large picture window, actually made up of twin, double-glazed windows, each with a golden-handled transom above two casements. Gauzy voile curtains are drawn over them, overlaid in turn with pale yellow velvet drapes hanging from a brass rod. Beneath is a rather sizable Simair radiator. Beyond the walkway that gives access to the rooms, the windows overlook a small courtyard: windows and a tile roof are visible on the other side. Planters full of pink geraniums line the guardrail along the walkway.

In the corner of the room facing the door is a round table mounted on a single leg with four little feet, and three wooden chairs upholstered in beige floral print. A brass chandelier made up of a central sphere from which radiate five curved candle-holders hangs from the ceiling. Beneath the chandelier is a circular blue wool rug with whitish-pink arabesques running through it. To the left of the bed, a small rectangular rug displays the same motifs, in the same colors. And that's all (which is already a lot).

Text handwritten on pages torn from Fragments, *by Armand Robin, published by Gallimard.*

7

Room 201, Botânico Residencial, bairro de São José 11, Coimbra:

The door opens onto a little entryway bordered on the left by a closet and by the bathroom on the right. The closet doors are of the same red polished-wood design—there being two. The floor is done in a light-colored polished parquet. Baseboards made of the same wood run along the walls, which measure about 4 meters, painted in a grainy light gray. The white ceiling is covered in plaster molding, also white.

The room itself, at the end of this little hallway, isn't very large: about 5 x 4 meters. A tall window, with casements enclosed by interior shutters of light wood, is deeply inset into the wall extending from the closets, and is draped in a thick, finely ribbed fabric flecked in gray. Against the wall underneath the window is a flat radiator (out of order, which is too bad, since it's cold and my mission requires that I remain immobile for long periods of time) and a luggage rack made of reddish wooden slats. An armchair upholstered in an ugly greenish gray fabric with copper stripes is set into the recess between the closet and the window.

The wall facing the door also has a window, identical in every way to the first (drapes, shutters, radiator . . .), to the left of which is a table made of dark red wood, with three drawers and fluted legs and holding a small Philips television set. On the wall above this is a mirror in a frame of the same wood: I spend the day staring at myself, sitting on a green plush-covered stool of the piano stool type. Not that I've turned into a narcissist, it's just that I have no other choice. Headphones over my ears, looking like a weary pilot, I work. Though it might not seem so, I'm in the process of preserving world peace (temporarily). In the mirror, I can see a bed made of dark red wood covered by a white damask bedspread behind me. On either side of the headboard, above which is framed some monstrosity meant to represent a vase of lilies, is a night table with a hurricane lamp equipped with an electric bulb, and on the right-hand table, an ivory Iwatsu touchtone telephone. To the right and left, and at the foot of the bed, are scattered rugs displaying foliage, birds, and deer framed in geometric motifs, in dominant tones of pea soup and burnt sienna. A bulky suspended fixture in porcelain and brass hovers overhead, like a jellyfish.

A transom set in varnished white wood, about two meters above the floor in the far wall, looks into the bathroom. Beneath, there is a dark wooden chair upholstered in the same green plush as my stool.

Thanks to various little hypersensitive devices buried in the wall behind the vase of lilies, I hear the slightest noise coming from the room adjacent to mine (a device quite similar to—but more highly perfected than—the one with which Marius, in *Les Misérables*, spies upon Thénardier, his neighbor in the Gorbeau shack). The occupant of room 202 is not a former innkeeper, but a former pilot for Air Portugal, a member of the brotherhood of bigots still nostalgic for *Doutor* Salazar and the little shepherdesses of Fatima. His addiction to gin, as well as the number of times his flight records contained a sighting of the Virgin Mary in the middle of the air, earned him first a demotion to ground crew, and eventually a pink slip—a misfortune that he blamed on the Bolsheviks who stirred up the abominable Carnation Revolution, and the Saracens who are still holding King Sebastian prisoner. I have no idea how the members of Al Qaeda got wind of this inconsequential matter, but however it happened, they had no trouble at all manipulating the childish and almost medieval mind of Fernando das Dores, convincing him to carry out a completely insane plan: to load a plane with a stock of religious trinkets purchased at Fatima and drop them over the pilgrims gathered at Mecca. One can only imagine the seething outrage all over the Muslim world when word of such an attack got out! Crucifixes, Blessed Virgins, Sacred Hearts of Jesus, the doves of the Holy Spirit, all raining down from the heavens upon the faithful gathered around the Kaaba! The Black Stone pelted with Crusader knickknacks! Jihad would surely set the planet ablaze, from the Philippines to Morocco. With the help of God, the world would be rid of the unbelievers once and for all.

It's to foil this Machiavellian plot that I find myself here in room 201 of the Botânico Residencial, bairro de São José in Coimbra. When I take a few minutes rest, I can see from my window, beneath the streetcar cables, the curve of a busy, sloping street. Black capes amble along the sidewalks, dragging tin cans attached to their feet: it's Latada day, the traditional student celebration. On the other side of the street, beneath billboards advertising the Chrysler PT Cruiser (*"Amor a primeira vista, paixão a segunda"*), an old slogan scrawled in red paint proclaims: *"Greve geral. Abaixo governo PS."* Further to the left is an elegant house with a white and yellow façade beneath a red-tiled roof, a loggia, and Manueline rope motifs. Beyond lies the Mondego Valley—or some valley, in any case, and a deep one at that. I gaze at this landscape, then I sit back down and put my headset back on, so I can spy on Fernando das Dores's ridiculous conversations. I stare wearily at my face in the mirror, discovering some fairly appalling details that I never noticed before. Thoughtfully, I pluck out my nose hairs, one by one.

> *Text handwritten on three sheets of airmail stationary bearing the letterhead "Hotel Tivoli/Lisboa."*

8

Room 207, Гостиница Аэрофлот (Hotel Aeroflot), Krasnoyarsk:

A good eight hours after leaving it, gradually coming to my
senses in the Chelyabinsk-Chita train, where they (who?) must
have tossed me like a mailbag, this is what I remember about
my room: the walls were denture pink (or better still, though it
amounts to the same thing, pink like the chewing-gum, which,
back when I was young, was called, and perhaps still is, "Mala-
bar") and the ceiling white. It was almost a suite: a little hallway
(with a closet on the left-hand side, and on the right a coatrack
and a refrigerator, atop which is an electric kettle) leading to a
"living room" furnished with an armchair and a couch upholstered in chestnut plush. Out the window, one could see a rather
squalid-looking kind of square, with several bus stops, and to
the left, the *aerovokzal,* the station for the airport bus, built in
the classic style of the Stalin era (in fact, elegantly kitschy), that
is, with a central campanile topped by a slender spire, like the
Peter and Paul Fortress or the Admiralty in Saint Petersburg.
I seem to recall that on the left in this living room there were
glass doors that opened into the actual bedroom. Most of this
room was in turn taken up by a couple of twin beds covered by
yellowish brown and white bedspreads, as far as I can . . . Well, I
wouldn't swear to it. The window here looked out onto the same
landscape.

Even though a few details of the room have come back, I can't for the life of me remember—no matter how hard I try—what I'm supposed to be doing here in Krasnoyarsk, and, more precisely, in the Aeroflot Hotel. All I know is that I got outrageously drunk, but apart from that? I seem to recall Ilyuchinsk being with me (and Pyotr, his kid brother, much the same sort of guy, a biologist working for the KGB). So, this all (my presence in Krasnoyarsk) might have something to do then with the business of the supposed cloned mammoths that the two brothers—in cahoots with Crook—are trying to sell to an American theme park. It's another of Gricha's schemes. He claims that by using the remains of ancient pachyderms, which are abundant in Siberia, he's capable of cloning a brand new one. Modern science, he likes to say, emphasizing this cryptic statement with a vague hand gesture. I'd like to know what his idea of modern science is . . . And at some point that evening, didn't I hang out with a redheaded whore named Tania? Given my state, nothing much could have happened.

Ah, it just occurred to me that there was an amazing curtain on the living room window, all gathered up and crimped, partly raised, canopied, pinkish purple, looking like Madame Pompadour's underwear. And from the ceiling there hung a three-lamp light fixture, a pseudo-countrified look. The floor was tiled in fake wood linoleum, brownish yellow. In short, an exquisite ensemble, as you can imagine. Through the train compartment window, snowy plains roll by, crisscrossed by dark woodlands and silver birch. A crumpled piece of paper in my pocket, with an address written in ballpoint pen: *улица Марама* 13. 13 rue Marat. Now what's that supposed to mean?

Text handwritten on pages torn from Dondog, *by Antoine Volodine, published by Seuil.*

9

Room 1908, ANA Hotel, 7-20 Naka-machi, Naka-ku, Hiroshima:

The door, lacquered in white, fitted with a peephole and chain, opens onto a hall of about 3.5 x 1 meters. The floor is a thick gray and white carpet, the wallpaper is an imitation fabric of thin stripes in the same tones, and the ceiling, about 3 meters high, is covered in cream linen paper. On the left, the bathroom door, coated in a grainy cream paint, is set in a brushed aluminum frame. The right-hand wall extends into the room proper, which measures about 5 x 4 meters. Following the wall, one first comes upon a National brand trouser press, then a collapsible luggage rack made of burnished tubing with mauve straps, and finally a desk in dark wood set off by lighter struts at each corner, above which hangs a mirror measuring about 50 x 30 centimeters, in a blond wood frame, slightly curved at the top. I see myself in it: dark circles under the eyes, unshaven, beige linen shirt, gray cotton jacket. Acceptable, for once. Arranged on the desktop are the following: a lamp with a round brass base, wood and brass stem, and white petticoat shade; a large Hitachi electric kettle; a tiny plastic shelf containing some tea bags and a couple of packets of Caffé Greco coffee. In one of the drawers, a small booklet labeled *Information on What to Do in Case of a Disaster:* great title. In front of the desk sits a rectangular stool on casters, like a piano stool, upholstered in a washed-out green. Beyond the desk, a cabinet-like piece, also in dark wood with lighter wood struts, without doors, holding a minibar on the bottom shelf and a Toshiba television on the top.

The wall facing the entryway has a window, measuring about 1.5 x 1.5 meters, set about sixty centimeters above the floor, with plate glass in a brushed aluminum sash; only the right-hand side opens, so you can air out the room. An aluminum shutter bears a sticker that reads: *Please refrain from throwing any article from the window for safety.* They're probably right, I guess. Voile curtains and double draperies printed in bronze and sepia vertical stripes are strung over the window. The luminous rectangles of hundreds of windows light up the night outside, as well as skyscrapers crowned in a red glow, a couple of illuminated billboards, the slightly darker silhouette of distant hills, and cars gliding along two stretches of avenue. To the left, a rather tall, six-sided building, in almost total darkness except for a few rectangles of bluish neon and its ruby crest of lights, blocks the view of the A-bomb Dome. Beyond the dome are the floodlight towers of the baseball stadium at Aioi Dori, and further still, a tower of metal latticework reminiscent of the top of (for example) an American battleship at Pearl Harbor.

Along the third wall, above a little table in dark wood edged in a lighter hue, and an armchair upholstered in a peas-and-carrots purée-colored diamond pattern, hangs a lithograph numbered 78/100, entitled *Overcast Sky,* depicting God knows what, a forest of green wheat—or spear-shaped trees—beneath a sky streaked bluish-red.

The headboard of the bed abuts the fourth wall, where the bathroom is. It is made from the same assembly of dark and light wood as the rest of the woodwork in the room, with two brown plastic-covered pads extending horizontally across the pillow area, and, to the left, a built-in radio-alarm clock in brushed aluminum. On the side table there's an ivory telephone and a brass reading lamp in a trapezoidal shade. A little laminated sign offers *Massage service, dial 73 for reservation ¥ 3000 for 30', ¥ 4500 for 45', ¥ 6000 for 60'.* The bed, about 1.5 x 2 meters, is covered with a bedspread in a green and beige grid pattern.

It isn't on this bed, however, that I am to frolic with Hisako, the beautiful captive, but rather on the red-and-blue striped carpeting in the elevator. She's the bell captain in the hotel lobby, and as soon as I laid eyes on her, I can't get her out of my thoughts—if you can call the obscene scenarios that seethe and stew in my loathsome brain, at a constant simmer, "thoughts." These sick fantasies of mine have her all tied up, a victim readied for sacrifice, as in Homer—game lashed to the saddle of a horse—vestal virgin and martyr—a despoiled ingénue out of Sade; anyway, you get my drift. Not that such fantasies are in any way unusual for me, but you also have to admit that the images of bondage, the classified ads that crowd the columns of Japanese newspapers—submissive high-school girls awaiting punishment, naughty nurses caught naked under their lab coats, brazen barmaids hoping to be humbled, that kind of thing— don't exactly paint you a picture of egalitarian, consensual sex. Not to mention the lucky assonance that allows for a slippage from "bell captain" to *"belle captive."* Hisako (I only learned her name once we were in the elevator) is petite, like a schoolgirl. You could easily wrap one hand around her neck. Her eyes—those strange, white-less Japanese eyes—are two tapering inky arrows; a few freckles dot her high cheekbones; and her mouth encloses tiny, close-set teeth (though large mouths are enticing, tiny ones can be sexy too; they remind me of a cruel story told by the writer Laszlo Düres, of a perverted feudal lord who had young girls delivered to him on the basis of their mouths being "no bigger than a hawthorn flower," so that the acts of fellatio they were forced to perform would cause them to die of suffocation). Hisako's hair, tied in a short ponytail at the back of her neck, is like a calligrapher's brush. She's wearing a navy blue skirt and a fitted lilac jacket, and a little pill-box hat with *"Belle Captive"* written on it in gold letters—in short, she's driving me crazy. So here we are, alone together in the elevator. I pray to God to let us get stuck, to turn this elevator into a dungeon for my beautiful captive. And just then, an earthquake measuring 6.5 on the Richter scale starts shaking Hiroshima. The lights go out, the elevator stops between the thirteenth and twelfth floors. I'm not feeling the least fear, but instead a keen exaltation (to put it politely). I'm God, I thought. I'm afraid, a small voice murmurs in the darkness. Don't be afraid, I say. I know what to do in case of a disaster. Hisako switches on the flashlight found in all hotel rooms and elevators, as a precaution in the event of exactly what's just taken place—or perhaps what's about to take place. Gently but firmly, I remove it from her hands and, bending over, folding her along with me, I place the lamp on the floor, in a corner of our cell. The beam lights up her helmet of dark hair, her obsidian eyes, silken legs, red flowers, and blue leaves.

Text handwritten on a sheet of stationary with the letterhead "ANA HOTEL HIROSHIMA," and two postcards ("Tokyo Station Hotel" and "Mt Fuji and Shinkansen Line").

10

Room 4, Hotel L'Andréa, 39 Avenue Jean-Jaurès, Brive:

The door opens directly onto a hallway-bathroom, whose floor, to the right (along with that of the room itself), is tiled in imitation parquet linoleum, whereas the bathroom itself, on the left, is done in nondescript, soupy white tile veined with gray and ochre, set about 2 meters higher than the floor in the bedroom. The door to the toilet faces the front entrance. To the left, in the tiled area, an oval sink and chrome faucet, over which hangs a rectangular mirror lit by a fluorescent tube. I stand in front of this mirror several times a day to brush my teeth, taking care not to dislodge the plastic tooth that replaces the right upper incisor, broken off by the safety catch of a hand grenade during an old street riot.[1] A blue pitcher is set on the countertop. On the left, a pinkish shower curtain provides a makeshift screen for the shower stall.

You enter the bedroom, to the right, by going down two steps. The room is about 5 x 5 meters. The ceiling, about 3 meters high, is painted white. Two of the walls (the one on the left as your enter, then the one it joins at a right angle, with a window) are roughcast in off-white, while the other two are hung in some kind of plastic fabric printed in a pattern of somewhere between fleur-de-lis and palmetto. To the left as you enter, there's a combination bench/luggage rack in laminate daubed in

---

1   During the events mistakenly attributed to "'68." *(AN)*

yellow, where an ochre bowl and a white pot full of nasturtiums have been set. Above this, a small watercolor under glass, unattractive, showing a manor house in a leafy landscape.

Against the wall there's a small heater (seven cast-iron heating elements), above which two boards on racks make up shelves. Between all this and the window hangs a hideous painting of a snowy village scene (as far as I can make it out). The window has two panes in a vinyl frame, white lace curtains, and wooden shutters painted white. Part the curtains, and you discover Rue Jean-Jaurès, with Rue Firmin-Marbeau jutting off at a sharp angle. Just to the left, a neon sign announces, in blue on white, horizontally: "Restaurant," and above, vertically: "Hotel." Houses in stone masonry with slate roofs, gray with white shutters. The red awning of the L'Andréa dripping beneath the window, the one at the hotel-bar Le Progrès—where Rue Firmin-Marbeau and Rue Jean-Jaurès come to a point—the one-way sign on the Rue Marbeau, all add spots of poppy red to the otherwise gray background. A two-light streetlamp set in a bed of yellow chrysanthemums is planted in the triangle formed where the aforementioned streets join.

The third wall contains a makeshift closet made out of laminate, without a door, in which an orange plastic, star-studded wastepaper basket has been placed. On the wall, a gouache on paper without a frame showing pink and white flowers against a blue background: "rather roughly executed, most definitely, but not so bad, not so bad, expressive even," Raymonde Docteur-Roux told me, adjusting her lorgnette. "What do you think, darling?" Raymonde Docteur-Roux had insisted on seeing my room. "A bit rustic, but it has its charms," she assessed. "And the parquet is simply splendid," she added, pointing to the linoleum. I was due to have a meeting in this inconspicuous hotel with Raymonde Docteur-Roux and three of her associates at the Kangaroo Prize: Jules Nourrisson, Paul Tabatière and a third whose name escapes me, Pâtissier or something like that.[2] We were there to negotiate the conditions in exchange for which I would be awarded the prize (this sentence, I grant you, is a bit awkward, an awkwardness that . . . that attests to my discomfort at stating the unvarnished truth. So, I may as well just put my foot in it: we were haggling over the purchasing price of the prestigious Kangaroo Prize). Docteur-Roux, Nourrisson, Tabatière, Tapissier (let's say), and myself are staying in five of the hotel's eight rooms. Naturally, my publisher's attorney was also present, but since this particular attorney happened to be a woman, and a good-looking one at that, we were sharing the same room (#4). So as not to attract attention, the bodyguards of Docteur-Roux, Nourrisson, etc., were being put up in the dormitory of a local summer camp. It was over a cup of tea in the lounge (if the name applies) of the L'Andréa that we talked business. "If someone had told me that one day I'd be drinking Lipton brewed from a tea bag . . ." simpered Raymonde. "Here, dear, it's all yours," she added, waving her lorgnette in my direc-

---

2 The author is poking fun at the names of certain members of the Goncourt Jury, which decides France's most prestigious yearly literary prize. *(Translator's Note)*

tion. Her cohorts kept their mouths shut, nodding their heads, hands crossed over their vests, inoffensive. When they did pipe up, it was only to make vociferous comments on the price of foie gras in the stores, or about the winter train schedule, which was about to go into effect—in any case, matters that have nothing to do with anything. One of them, startled awake by his cell phone, proceeded to remove a small pocket calculator from his jacket and, sticking it stubbornly to his ear, grumbled to the person at the other end to speak up, goddamn it, he couldn't hear a word. Don't fall for it, the attorney said, they're not the least bit stupid. That's all just an act to lull us into complacency. I don't really remember much about them, now; seems to me that one was bald, another had a beard, and one was hard of hearing, but I wouldn't swear to it.

The bed frame, made out of blue metal tubing, is up against the fourth wall and covered by a down comforter colored a rather intense orange and mauve. Two sconces of pinkish porcelain, each mimicking the shape of half a water lily, are fixed to the wall on either side. It's under this bed that the Delsey suitcase full of cash was stashed. I don't remember the price we were settling on, but it was no bargain. Still, the talks never got anywhere. On the second day, taking advantage of my attorney's absence when she went off to flirt with Tabatière (or was it Nourrisson?) in the hope of getting a discount, I snuck off with the suitcase. I needed the money to pay the ransom for Mélanie Melbourne, the love of my life, whom Islamist terrorists were holding prisoner somewhere in the desert. Iskandar Arak-Bar, a Syrian poet friend of mine, full-time alcoholic and part-time double agent, acted as my go-between with them (stage-managed, perhaps— at least that's my suspicion—by Antonomarenko, who was hoping to get a cut; and it's quite likely that all this had more than a little to do with the bastard's—allegedly mysterious—death in a Buenos Aires hotel room. I've got my own ideas on the matter, but that's a different subject, which I'll address another time).

So, there you have it. That's how I missed out on the prestigious Kangaroo Prize. I can say that it was for a good cause.[3]

Text typed out on two A4-size sheets of paper.

---

3 There exists a variant—or rather a complication—of this story, which states that the Ansar al-Islam group, which had kidnapped Mélanie Melbourne and was holding her prisoner, had in fact been bribed by a rival publisher to do so: aware of my feelings for her, this publisher is thought to have figured (a guess that proved correct) that I would do what I ended up doing, and therefore that the deal with the Kangaroo jury, the deal that we were on the verge of "wrapping," as they say these days, would collapse at the last minute. The intelligence I've managed to gather on this affair isn't enough as yet to confirm or deny this inspired premise. Still, I refuse to believe that people engaged, granted, in a business—but *intellectual* business, after all—could stoop to such base tactics. *(AN)*

Room 503, Hotel Opera, 37 Strada Brezolanu, sector 5, Bucharest:

Now, this is a complicated room, hard to describe . . . Very complicated, even. But then Romania isn't an easy country. I don't know if this is going to make sense. The front door, in brown wood, opens into a hallway bordered on the left by the bedroom wall, and on the right by that of the bathroom. The walls are painted pale yellow, the ceiling robin's egg blue, the carpet sky blue printed with gray squares. Along the right-hand wall, first of all, beneath the white grillwork of the Henderson air-conditioner, is a collapsible baggage rack of chrome tubing with black straps. Next comes the Episcopal door (purple, with a golden handle) to the bathroom. After that, about 3.5 meters from the entrance, the wall makes a sharp turn on the right-hand side, creating a little alcove that features a low circular glass-topped table in a metal frame, mounted on a three-footed stand and bearing a phial and an ashtray, as well as a little dresser made of blond wood, consisting of four drawers with gilt metal handles. At the back of the alcove is a sliding glass door, about 2 meters high and .5 meters wide, set in a black metal frame, opening onto a little balcony tiled in pink.

The wall facing the front door is taken up almost entirely by a horizontal picture window measuring about 1 meter high and 2.5 meters long, in a black metal frame. All along the window, and the French doors as well, are strung yellowish voile curtains and double drapes covered in blue and white stripes and sprinkled with geometric shapes. From the balcony and the picture window, one can see the intersection of Brezolanu, Victor-Eftimiu, and Demetriade-Aristide Streets, and in the distance, Ion-Campineanu Street, with its square and colonnades of the museum. Cars (especially Dacias), dirty gray buildings (including the one bearing the inscription APA BUCURESTI, Bucharest Water, in blue letters), and orange lampposts. On Campineanu, past Apa Bucuresti, is an eighteen-story apartment block, like the ones in cheap housing projects. Eftimiu Street, which is rather narrow and passes right below the balcony and the picture window, runs toward Cismigiu Park, whose dark foliage is visible some one hundred meters away. Orange lights are suspended down the middle of the street by a system of catenaries. There's only one lit window on any of the six floors in the building across the street, bright and slightly open, a little lower than mine: the raw neon light reveals a cluttered desk (mineral water and orange juice bottles, rolls of paper, a computer, a swivel chair in imitation black leather). A young and apparently athletic guy, in a short-sleeved black T-shirt, medium length blond hair, is sitting in the swivel chair. Down in the street, two guys in shirtsleeves are sitting in white plastic chairs. Somewhere in the night, a dog is barking endlessly.

The space between a large pillar and the wall to the left of the entrance gives access to the actual bedroom, which measures approximately 4.5 x 4.5 meters. Set in the angle formed by the pillar and the front wall is an armchair upholstered in white fabric with little blue motifs, the same as the draperies. Hanging above it is a framed sepia photograph of pre-war Bucharest. Adjacent is another horizontal picture window just like the one mentioned above, with the same curtains, and the same view onto the same Victor-Eftimiu Street.

The two twin beds abut the wall at a right angle to the one I've just described. Tall headboards in an oak-like wood. White bedspreads with blue stripes (matching the other stripes in the drapes, it's all so complicated . . .). Two cubical night tables with double drawers each bear a gold metal lamp with a white fabric shade on a fluted stand. On the table furthest to the left (in the corner made with the other wall) there's also an Alcatel telephone. On the wall above, between the two beds, is another sepia photograph, larger this time, of bygone Bucharest: Patriarchy Hill, to be exact.

The wall facing the bay window is bare, except for still another large sepia photograph in the middle, depicting an exclusively male crowd, all wearing bowler hats and carrying umbrellas—which are probably parasols, come to think of it, because it seems to be very sunny out—all crowding in front of buildings decked with flags. The far wall, cordoning off the hallway, has a mirror framed in the same oak-like wood. Beneath it, a desk, again made of the same wood, holding a built-in minibar, a Philips TV, a chrome tray with two cups, two glasses, an electric kettle and box of tea bags, and finally a lamp in gilded metal like the one described above.

In the lighted office down below, the athlete with the medium length blond hair, whose black short-sleeved T-shirt reveals arms the size of hams, is rotating in nervous half circles from right to left, then from left to right, in his imitation leather swivel chair. While doing so, he compulsively squeezes and releases a kind of spring-loaded grip designed to build muscle strength in the hand. His flat head makes him instantly recognizable: it's Medusa, the Lipovan hatchet man. To tell about the circumstances of my first meeting with this shady character would get me too far off track; that will be the topic of another story (maybe). Under the present circumstances, I've no time to reminisce. All I know is that I've got to prevent him from killing Mélanie Melbourne, my shy and ever-endangered love. She sure loves putting herself in the lion's jaws. This inclination for calamity can be annoying—even disheartening—but I interpret it as her way of offering me multiple opportunities to prove my love. Mélanie must still love me as long as she continues to put herself in harm's way just so I can rescue her: the ultimate in generosity! This thought causes me to shed a tear, which I wipe away with the back of my hand. This is no time for clouded vision. Slowly, hiding behind the blue-and-white striped draperies of room 503, I load my Glock 17. That dog is still barking.

Text handwritten on pages torn out of Moravagine, *by Blaise Cendrars, published by Denoël.*

Room 402, Dan Chu Hotel, 29 Phô Trang Tien, Hanoi:

The square, spacious room measures about 7 x 7 meters. The ceiling, with a heavy molding forming a cornice, is about 4 meters high. The molding gathers into a rosette at the center—no doubt the trace of a long-gone chandelier. The walls and ceilings are painted in off-white, and the parquet floor is a mahogany tone. The door is set in an arched panel framed by two Doric pilasters, with the whole thing—door, panel, and pilasters—painted in a dark lacquer, almost black. A wide floorboard made of the same dark wood runs all along the bottom of the walls. The door is set into an otherwise bare wall. On the outside, it opens onto the end of an open-air gallery.

A console made of brown wood, with two shuttered doors and housing the minibar, sits in the corner, against the left-hand wall. There's a Samsung television set on top. Next, on a blue porcelain pedestal in the shape of an eggcup, there's a cylindrical bluish plastic container of Tan Viên mineral water. The "window" is made up of a panel in dark wood framed by pilasters, etc., in exactly the same design as the door. No glass panes: it's a full door that opens onto a small tiled balcony whose guard rail is placed dangerously low. To the left, Trang Tien Street comes into view, with the façade, covered in blue netting, of the Alliance Française undergoing renovation. Further on, a couple of modern buildings, cumbersome and ugly, most notably the

VIETCOMBANK building, burgundy with green windows (an unintended illustration of the "raw apple and red wine" vomit, studied—if we are to believe Boris Vian—by Jean-Sol Partre). In front, beyond a little street lined with trees and utility pylons bearing an extremely unkempt system of insulators and transformers, are trees and roofs: double-pitched red tile colonial roofs, corrugated metal painted deep red, or flat terraced roofs on postmodern giraffe houses.[1] Shiny metal cylindrical cisterns, dish antennae. Further away, the cream-colored balusters, the griffons, the turrets, and the slate rooftops of the Grand Theater, over which flies the red flag with the lone gold star. To the right of that is the hideously over-inflated, pomo, Bofillesque Hilton Hotel, which culminates in a horrendous blind wall topped with a nearly isosceles pediment and framed by two Dorico-Babylonian columns. The architect of this piece of shit is a *Phap,* a Frenchman, so it seems, a certain Claude Cuvelier (may he drink boiling water!). Further to the right, the pagoda-style tiled roofs of the old university, built by the same architect as the former French School of the Far East (Hébrard). That's where I'll have to operate from in a little while. Anyone who weighed the Hilton against the old university would undoubtedly conclude that architecture (and concomitantly, aesthetics) took a great leap backwards when the neo-socialist style replaced that of the colonial days. Right under my window, in the little street that runs beneath the balcony, workers are erecting the brick walls of a house. Trowel in hand and balanced on two-by-fours, a couple

---

1   ? *(EN)*

of them are wearing *bô-doï* caps. Red, white, and blue striped tarps (like shopping bags from a Tati department store) protect all openings. The vast cackle of car engines and horns. Beyond the window, two round wicker chairs with white cushions flank a wickerwork stand with a circular glass tabletop, on which there's a blue patterned porcelain cup and dish, a bud vase containing a rose, an ashtray, and a lotus-shaped candle holder with a thin taper stuck in it.

The door to the bathroom is in the wall facing the entrance: a large pane of frosted glass rounded off on top, in dark wood frame. Above it, the air-conditioner. To the left, a jacket stand in white lacquer and a baggage rack in dark wood, the top of which is covered in light red carpet. To the right, a double-door wardrobe in russet wood.

Against the fourth wall—the one facing the window, that is—is the oversized bed, whose frame and ornamented posts are in reddish wood. No bedspread, but rather a blanket in a blue-white-orange pattern. On either side, chunky single-drawer night tables in the same satin-finished red wood, with a lamp on each, each with a gold metal base, a blue porcelain stem, and a red shade. On the wall above, two intricately cut glass sconces with pendants. Next, a two-drawer table of the same red wood that looks almost like plastic, and a chair of the same wood, with a cushion covered in a rough green fabric. Above the table, a mirror framed in the same plastic-looking wood, in which I see reflected—behind my tanned face where two eyes shine nearly yellow—the Babylonian outline of the Hilton, spinach-green trees, and beneath an overcast sky, the pagoda roofs of what was once the university where, in two hours (I check my watch) . . .

Two hours later, disguised (overcoming my reluctance) as a typical Western tourist (walking shoes, shorts, fanny pack, backpack, T-shirt, dark glasses, pith helmet), I climb the stairs located behind the main building of the former university, on Lê-Thanh-Tông. Lined up in rows, the students are doing calisthenics in the courtyard (I can't help ogling some of the graceful girls, fine bones like spun glass, but only furtively, on the move, out of the corner of my eye: this is no time to attract attention). At the top of the stairs, a dusty mammoth skeleton seems to be waiting to welcome me to the Natural History Museum, which hasn't been open in years. I knock at the door, three short and two long, as agreed. I hear tiny footsteps, then the sound of sliding bolts. The cleaning lady, a gauze mask over her mouth, opens the door, steps aside to let me in; I enter, she closes the door behind me and slides the bolts back into place. It's full of skeletons, large and small, yellowish in the dim light, many only half complete. There are stuffed animals, skinned and scraped, eaten away by mites, their mummified guts visible under the exposed weft. Birds and insects fly around among these ruins. Without a word, sliding along in her slippers, the cleaning lady leads me to the skeleton of a large Borneo orangutan (*simia satyrus*). Yeah, right. Well, I happen to know that it's Lieutenant Colonel Terry Anderson, native of Tampa, Florida, shot down on the 9th of August 1967 aboard his Phantom jet while fleeing a battery of SAM missiles in the Haiphong region. His family, wealthy hotel magnates, are offering a million dollars to anyone who recovers his remains. The Vietnamese authorities deny ever capturing Anderson—the hole in the back of his skull proves he's been murdered, execution style. It was Arlette Harlow, a former mistress of mine, heiress (among other things) to the Colgate toothpaste fortune, who put me onto the deal. Did it interest me? You bet it did! I needed money to get Mélanie Melbourne out of trouble, since she'd managed once again to get herself into a real fix. But that's another story. Gricha Ilyuchinsk put me in touch with some of the more easily bribed top brass in the People's Army—an army where there's plenty of people wanting to be bought. And that's how I find myself, on this late afternoon, in front of the skeleton of Terry Anderson. With a couple of snips of my wire cutters, I sever the frame that holds up the so-called orangutan, and in a few seconds, I empty the bones into my backpack. It's in the bag—we're in the money! Comrade cleaning lady, into whose hand I've just stuffed five twenty-dollar bills, is pretending to busy herself, somewhat negligently, with dusting off a kind of prehistoric dromedary.

How I managed to get the lieutenant colonel's remains out of Vietnam is another story, which I will tell, perhaps, if you're good. It starts in the old town, on Phô-Hang-Bac, the street where coffin makers and headstone engravers do business. I know, by the way, that certain people accuse me of swindling the Anderson family (and the Natural History Museum along with them) by making off with the skeleton of an actual orangutan—an allegation I simply shrug off. Do they think that people ready to pay *cash on the barrel and in full* (I must emphasize) for a bag of bones don't have the wherewithal to pay for DNA tests? Leaving behind such tedious debates, I would rather point out one last feature of room 402: it is frequently visited by little black *mini-gators.* You probably call them geckos. But I call them *mini-gators.* Comes from my childhood in Africa.

> *Text handwritten on two pages torn from* Tales of Mystery and Imagination *by Edgar Allan Poe, Gallimard, Folio Collection, and on the back of two post-cards* ("Ha Long, a Boat-wharf" *and* "Ha Noi, Luong-Van-Can Street").

– 13 –

Room 211, Hotel Crystal, 5 rue Chanzy, Nancy:

Nothing. There was a box of macaroons from the Macaron Sisters on the desk, and a collapsible luggage rack. That's all I remember. I don't think I ate a single one (of the macaroons, I mean). I think . . . could I have kept them as a present for Mélanie Melbourne?

> *Text handwritten on the back of a "Menu/Departure Singapore" from an Air France flight* (Poulet tandoori achard de legumes et ananas / *Tandoori chicken with pineapple achard;* Sauté de boeuf sauce riz rouge / *Braised beef in red rice sauce;* Kai lan, riz cantonais / *Kai lan, fried rice;* ou / *or* Ragoût de perche et saumon sauce homardine / *Perch and salmon ragout in Lobster sauce;* Pommes vapeur, broccolis / *Steamed potatoes, broccoli;* Fromage / *Cheese;* Mousse chocolat-framboise / *Chocolate and raspberry mousse; Café de Colombia).*

– 14 –

Room 409, Hotel Cavalier, Rue Mohammed-Abdel-Baki, Hamra, Beirut:

The door is pale brown Havana wood, fitted with a peephole, and it opens onto a small hallway measuring about 3 x 1 meters. On the right, the double doors of the closet, in light brown Havana wood with two little golden balls as handles; and on the left, the golden-handled door of the bathroom.

The carpet is dark blue, with a pattern of little mauve squares. The walls and ceiling (about 3 meters high) are painted cream. At the center of the ceiling, a rose light fixture in frosted glass. The room itself is a 5 meter cube. Along the right-hand wall as you enter is a luggage rack made out of the same wood as all the rest, with a Plexiglas cover riveted to the wall for protection, then a desk that's not much more than a plank of wood set at a dihedral angle to a dresser with two drawers and two doors. A rectangular stool upholstered in an orange, checkered fabric allows one to sit in front of the desk—in order, for example, to gaze into the square, unframed mirror affixed to the wall above it at eye level. The sight reflected back, it must be said, is rather grim: last night, until the dawn call to prayer (may God forgive me), I got completely drunk in the company of Papadiamantides and Arak-Bar. What I see in the mirror sitting atop my shoulders is a wrinkly, reddish sack—a mushy, wine-soaked pear—crested with scarce, bristling strands of hair and pitted with two plague-ridden rat's eyes. Next is a black minibar with a glass door, displaying the items inside (there's nothing left but mineral water and fruit juice now), and a Sony television set on top. Then, in the corner with the windowed wall, a wooden table topped with glass, resting on a black iron stand, as well as an armchair upholstered in the same checkered orange fabric as the stool, and a rather squat armchair. On the wall above it, a brass sconce illuminates a little watercolor showing an oriental, latticework balcony and some cypress trees: a classic view.

The back wall is taken up entirely by the three large plate-glass windows—the center pane slides open—set in a metal frame painted cream. There are sheer white curtains and dark blue drapes with a flower (tulips) and fruit pattern, in pale green and orange, rather pretty. The window looks onto a balcony 1.75 meters wide, tiled in beige with an aluminum guardrail over-looking Mohammed Abdel Baki Street. To the left, Hamra Street, bustling, with the United Bank of Saudi & Lebanon Building, where the funds from the transaction should be deposited (after passing through the Caiman Islands). That is, if the transaction ever took place: after last night's goings-on, alas, all bets are off. To the right, a small parking lot, a palm tree, some buildings. Across the street, a building with darkened windows—except for one, directly opposite my balcony, still coated with anti-shatter window gauze, through which I can make out a faintly lit room. Now, at this moment—it's 6 P.M.—the muezzin's call to prayer sounds. Call away, pal.

In the corner between the back and the third wall, behind

the armchair, a copper-stemmed floor lamp supports a white shade. Behind that, a little watercolor, of the same quality as the other, representing a little street with an archway and a door. The two beds, about 1.5 meters wide, are set against rectangular headboards in brown Havana wood, about 4 x 1 meters. Swivel lamps with copper stems and white shades are affixed to the wall above each. The beds are covered with quilted spreads in a blue striped fabric with a pattern close to that of the drapes, but not exactly: I realize this as I concentrate on each design in the dim hope of forgetting the tungsten drills boring through my cranium. Between the two beds, there's a little one-drawer night table, topped with another glass shield, in light brown Havana wood.

On the fourth wall (where the bathroom is located), lit by a copper sconce, is a large, ugly watercolor in insipid blue and muddy maroon, portraying the ever-popular restaurant terrace at the port of Byblos. This picture is doubly disgusting to me: because it's ugly, and because it was there, in Byblos—on that same terrace—that we blithely embarked upon our disastrous evening: Themistocles Papadiamantides, Iskandar Arak-Bar and myself (I take my shirt and drape it over this eyesore, to get it out of my sight). It was after Byblos that things took a turn for the worse, when we went over to the Armenian's. There, we spent the evening talking about God knows what (poetry, perhaps), munching on carrots, radishes, and cucumbers and downing pitchers of arak. After taking our leave of the Armenian, just when—as I said previously—the call to dawn prayer rang out, Themistocles cracked his head open by walking through a plate glass door at the Café de Paris, on the corner of Hamra Street. I believe he must have hailed a taxi, then, with Iskandar, to get back to the port. I don't actually have any memory of this, but it seems plausible. As for me, I slept fully clothed, my teeth planted in the dark blue carpet, flecked in mauve, of room 409.

Themistocles rechristened *Agapè* (which means *Love*) the little freighter he bought from a supposedly Bahamian shipper, and had it licensed at Limassol. Odd name, given the kind of freight it's carrying: three hundred tons of Semtex, enough to flatten Manhattan. Though, in reality, it isn't Semtex at all—just modeling clay. Iskandar's the one who put us onto the deal, and at present (while the muezzin continues his chanting), I wonder whether we should really be grateful to him. He learned from his contacts in the secret services that the ingenious Czech engineer Pavel Schmelk had developed a modeling clay that perfectly replicated the consistency, color, and odor of Semtex (even dogs were fooled): the only difference is that it doesn't explode. So, one thing leading to another, we struck a deal with a branch of the CIA (for a handsome reward, it should be said) to carry out an assignment that, as of tonight, has started looking more and more like a suicide mission: to load three hundred tons of the fake stuff in Trieste *for real*, make a stopover in Beirut in order to *fictitiously* load the same amount of the real thing, and then head to the Indian Ocean to sell the stuff to the Tamil Tigers, who'll then resell it, after taking their commission, to the Indonesian branch of Jamaa Islamiya. It looked like a straightforward deal. "Emballez, c'est pesé," Iskandar repeated incessantly (who, as an occasional translator of Mallarmé and Maeterlinck into Arabic, possessed a purportedly "common" French vocabulary that was delightfully archaic). It promised an exceptionally good return on our investment (we're going to be rolling in it, Iskandar twittered). Except for one thing: there are still two crates of *real* Semtex in the hold, so as to allow for a demonstration, upon delivery, to our clients, who we must assume are not fools. Fanatics, to be sure, but not fools. Now, listen carefully: we have three hundred tons divided into six thousand crates weighing fifty kilos apiece, each bearing an ID painted in black, composed of two letters and three numbers. As a security measure, I'm the only one—as head of the operation—who knows the ID numbers of the two crates containing the real Semtex. Or rather, I used to be, because last night's binge made me forget them. And I mean completely. Of course, I remember that there was some mnemonic device, but what was it? You've probably tried tapping away randomly at a keypad in the hope of getting a door with an electronic lock to open: well, that's more or less the situation I'm in, but far more dangerous. If you get any bright ideas, let me know.

> *Text handwritten on two sheets of stationary adorned with a stylized Greek warrior (helmet, shield, and spear), "Hotel Alexander / Adib-Ishak Street / Beirut."*

– 15 –

Room 413, Hotel Шереметьево 2 (Sheremetyevo 2), Moscow-Sheremetyevo Airport:

The front door, made out of plywood, is equipped with a handle that dangles loosely from poorly fitted screws. It opens onto a hallway measuring about 2.5 x 1 meters, with a closet, also in plywood, on the left-hand side, and on the right, papered over in imitation marble, the door to the bathroom. Walls painted in denture pink and a mottled carpet in brown/pink (these descriptors apply to the whole room). Above the front door, there's a square light fixture in frosted plastic that illuminates the hallway. To the left, facing the door, there's a bare electrical fixture where there was once a doorbell—quite a rarity in a hotel room.[1]

A second plywood door opens onto the room itself, which measures about 5.5 x 4 meters. Ceiling 3 meters high, painted in white. Two fire sprinklers will remind anyone with a good political memory of the bugging devices that these artifacts were supposed to conceal in the hotels of the USSR (Pavel Schmelk invented a system—inspired, so it seems, by that tiny barbed Amazonian fish that supposedly swims up the stream of your piss to lodge itself in the urethra[2]—which had the effect of in-

[1]   But in a Russian hotel room, anything is possible. *(AN)*
[2]   This story of the barbed fish swimming up an Amazonian pisser's stream, like a spawning salmon—is it true or is it completely made up? I have no idea (but I'm inclined to opt for the latter). *(AN)*

verting the eavesdropping flow: fitted with a Schmelk air valve microphone, the fire sprinkler would no longer transmit conversations to the KGB, but instead would make it possible for the room's occupants to pick up the KGB's obnoxious private noises: veritable burping, farting, and snoring contests, anti-Semitic jokes, idiotic sports forecasts, stoogery in all its forms.[3] In a sense, the system pumped *out* instead of drawing *in*.) Against the wall on the left as you enter is a little desk, a modern geometric design in black wood, flanked by two black tube chairs, with seats and backs in a greenish purple plush. In the corner of this wall and the one with the window, a small one-drawer chest in the same black-tinted wood, and on a shelf, a little Sharp TV.

In the wall facing the entrance is a double glazed casement window measuring about 1.5 meters high and .8 meter for each of the two panes,[4] highlighted by two florescent ceiling lights. Each pane is hung with lace curtains and pink velvet drapes. The view out the window is a minimalist landscape, typically—and dismally—Russian: patches of dirty snow residue, spattering the grass still scorched by winter, buildings in a state between unfinished and ruined, overhead pipelines[5] forming an archway over

---

3 Everyone talks about the Berlin Wall, Solidarity, Solzhenitsyn, Star Wars, etc., but no one knows about the role the Schmelk air valve microphones played in the collapse of the Soviet empire. And not only by revealing the mysteries of the Eastern Bloc's security system, but also by drying up its channels of information, thereby fostering an atmosphere of discouragement, disunity, and, in the end, of nihilism and drunkenness among the guard dogs of the Communist regime. *(AN)*

4 We have been told that the window frame is painted white. *(EN)*

5 And which one can reasonably presume to be broken. *(AN)*

a muddy road strewn with old Ladas, where a man in a raincoat[6] suddenly emerges running at full speed, pursued by two militiamen. Maybe the militiamen are making use of the Star pistols they're brandishing, but the noise of the planes taking off and landing at Sheremetyevo Airport makes it all but impossible to tell. Beyond, the landscape is bordered by a stand of birch trees, into which the fugitive and his pursuers soon disappear. Under the window, there's a radiator, the kind you find in cars. To the right of the window, in the corner made with the third wall, the same low, one-drawer chest in black holds a cut-glass ashtray. Abutting this wall is the bed, covered with a kind of plush spread in black/brown/purple stripes.[7] Above the head of the bed, a lamp with a frosted-gilded-festooned shade, looking like a jellyfish. In the corner made with the last wall (where the bathroom is located), sits a rather imposing, high-backed sofa: hideous, upholstered in the same indescribable plush.

One more thing: to the right of the door (if you face it), a little wall thermometer reads a temperature of . . . [8]

Text handwritten on two pages torn from Sakhalin Island *by Anton Chekhov, Gallimard, Folio Collection.*

---

6   Some have suggested that this was Pavel Schmelk, and this could well have been the case. But Pavel Schmelk died recently in a plane crash—as yet unexplained—in Mongolia, where he had gone to do some hiking. If the fugitive mentioned in this text is indeed the Czech engineer, then he must have eluded his pursuers. *(EN)*

7   The bed is very hard, but you can't really tell just by looking at it. *(AN)*

8   The text ends here, abruptly—either because something or someone made a sudden interruption, or, quite simply, because the pen ran out of ink. *(EN)*

Room 12, Villa Medici,[1] viale Trinitá dei Monti, 1, Rome:

The double doors, made of wood coated in old, peeling paint—somewhere between gunmetal gray and copper green—fitted with a large, horizontally sliding iron bolt, and a small, round brass doorknob, are located at the far end of an antechamber, where you'll also find the door to the bathroom, on the right. As for the room itself, it opens out from a deep embrasure. The left-hand wall of the room is about 1 meter away from the left-hand edge of the embrasure, while the wall on the right is about 5 meters from the right-hand edge. The lateral walls run about 12 meters each. The ceiling—composed of three recessed panels in ochre wood, straddled by nine joists crisscrossed with thinner struts, so that each panel is cut into fifty squares—is about 6 meters from the floor. So, you can imagine how enormous this room is.

The walls are unevenly whitewashed, creating a marbling effect, between beige, putty, and lime green. A gray faux facing edged in darker gray molding runs about 1 meter from the floor, which is done in large polished tiles of pale ochre. A fresco-like frieze, about a meter wide, runs just below the ceiling: land and seascapes, in tones tending toward blues and greens—

---

1   I've taken the liberty of including the Villa (the location of the Academy of France in Rome) in my hotel nomenclature simply because the room I occupy bears a number, I carry the key around with me in my pocket all day, and it's located in a city where I don't normally live. *(AN)*

Patinierian, I'd say, just to be pedantic—are surrounded by little cherubs and motifs inspired by the villas of Pompeii. The height of the room, and the shadow cast on the whole half of it at this late afternoon hour, make it hard to read the words, maxims or mottos, inscribed there in Latin: SUAVE, VICTORIA AMAT CURAM . . . Large rectangles of clear adhesive tape cover over some cracks.

Along the left-hand wall as you enter there are, in order: an armchair of medieval stiffness, a kind of throne upholstered in studded leather (the kind you can see in paintings by Jean-Paul Laurens; in fact, the whole room looks like a scene from some historical painting, like the *Excommunication of Robert the Pious*); a radiator in a recess; a combination chest / writing desk with three curved drawers—though the writing desk panel no longer opens; an iron candelabrum with a cylindrical white shade—the design that looks churchy to me, though I don't know why; the bed, made of wrought iron, standing quite high (perhaps 80 centimeters), covered with a rather pathetic spread in ochre terrycloth; and, at the foot of the bed, a huge bench upholstered in a threadbare green velvet. Next is the three-legged half-moon table in rustic wood (cherry?), holding a candelabrum in gilded wood on four lion's paw feet with a white cylindrical shade in ochre canvas, extremely churchy; then, in front of the table, a modern chair in gray tubing, the seat cushion in apricot velvet; and finally, in a recess corresponding to an old, sealed-off door, another throne chair of the type described above.

The back wall is hollowed out by an embrasure symmetrical

to that of the door, and of the same dimensions. Inside, at the back, is a square window made up of two panes divided into seven rows of three smaller panes set in lead, with wooden shutters measuring about 1.5 x 1.5 meters; vertically sliding iron bolts on the right-hand pane lock the window, which overlooks the Viale Trinitá dei Monti from a height of about 30 meters. To the left, you can see the church of the same name, from just about exactly the same angle that Corot painted it; then Quirinal Hill, Victor Emmanuel's wedding cake, or the typewriter, as it's often called; and the rooftops of Rome bristling with domes and cupolas, the Janiculum directly opposite, behind trees that glow red in the sunset, between a dome that might be Santi Ambrogio e Carlo al Corso and Saint Peter's; then, to the right, the heights of Mount Mario behind the cupolas of the twin churches of the Piazza del Popolo. A swarming of ochres, pinks, and blues, amid which lights begin to flicker on. The sky is red over the Janiculum, and then fades into a full palette of apricot and peach tones, culminating in Marian blue. Clouds of starlings merge and disperse acrobatically above the Vatican (like a shattered heart). Another throne chair, same as the other two, unless even more patently medieval, is set in front of the window, next to a rectangular table in rustic wood: heavy, rather ugly and impractical (impossible to cross your legs under it), fitted with a large drawer. The light cast by a second candelabra being a bit too dim, I set up a black articulated lamp (a so-called "architect's lamp") on the desktop, and it's by this light that I am attempting to compose the final paragraphs of my lecture "Plato in Proust," which I'm supposed to be delivering in less than two hours at the Saint-Louis Center. And I'm a little worked up. Because, on the one hand, the usual crowd at the Saint-Louis Center—a wing of the French diplomatic mission to the Vatican—is not exactly the type of audience I'm used to addressing. Stuffy old embassy bats and churchy clergymen. Men of the (scented) cloth, powdered old biddies, sagging skins in blazers, snoring bigots. I've even been told that a cardinal, very well versed in Augustinian thought, a Mgr. Fottorino, will be honoring me with his presence[2] (as for me, I accepted this invitation to Rome only because I knew that Pashmina Pachelbel, the queen of Turkish strippers, was going to be doing a show at the Coliseum: a gory recreation of some well-known Christian martyrdoms). But the main reason for my disquiet is that I discovered, about half an hour ago, that the itching I felt in my crotch was due to a thriving colony of crabs (a species that, for whatever reason, I had thought seriously endangered, or even completely extinct).

Except I've just realized that I didn't finish describing the room to you. Along the third wall (the one on the right-hand side as you enter), the following are arranged: a throne chair upholstered in leather, a very rustic-looking chest of drawers, peasant-meets-Louis XVI, let's say, in blond wood, with three drawers fitted with little brass handles; then, on the other side of the pink marble fireplace—somewhat stingily proportioned,

---

2   This fellow's presence didn't astonish me in the least, however, despite my feigned display of honored surprise—for reasons that I'll explain when the time comes. Perhaps. *(AN)*
(See "room" 31, Peacock Inn—EN)

given the size of the room—a rustic but attractive dresser, whose twin panels are painted in Roman floral motifs, flanked by two more throne chairs upholstered in a golden brown fabric. Along the fourth wall, coming back to the door, there's a rustic sideboard about 2.5 meters long, in dark wood, a convenient place to set suitcases; and a final throne chair upholstered in leather, behind which two panels with little brass knobs open onto a deep, empty niche.

As my eye wanders over all of this, which the setting sun bathes in Baudelairian colors, I realize that I no longer have enough time to run to the pharmacy, and that, anyway, I have no idea how the fuck to say "crabs" in Italian,[3] which is not the kind of language-related question one feels comfortable putting to the director of the Villa or to the cultural attaché of the embassy; and that, in any case, the over-the-counter treatments aren't fast-acting, when they act at all. So I'm going to have to lecture, in front of a cardinal, about the myth of the cave and literature as the unveiling of essences, with this itchy anthill here in my underwear. I'd like to see you do it. Any attempt to think, or even to feign thinking, inexorably returns me to my dilemma. You'd be worked up over far less, I should think.

> *Text handwritten on two sheets of stationary with* "Académie de France à Rome" *letterhead, and on two postcards (*"Carcere Mamertino" *and* "Guido Reni: Beatrice Cenci"*).*

---

3   *"Piottola." (EN)*

Room 211, Hotel Crystal, 5 Rue Chanzy, Nancy:

The front door . . . No. Don't go hoping you'll catch me out, it won't work. I told you that I didn't remember anything. There was a box of macaroons from the Macaron Sisters on the desk, and a collapsible luggage rack, that's all. I don't think I ate the macaroons. I may have given them to Mélanie Melbourne as a present, or in any case, that's what I should have done, and undoubtedly what I intended to do. And in the final analysis, it's highly probable that I did just that. I don't like macaroons, but even if it had been a matter of something I did like (bergamot candies, for instance, or Bordeaux *cannelé,* the kind of goodies hotel managements are accustomed to provide for their guests), I would still have given it to Mélanie Melbourne. I would have given anything and everything to Mélanie Melbourne. I have nothing further to declare.

> *Text handwritten on a Paris taxi receipt (fare 75 F, dated 3/21/1989).*

Room 309, Hotel Maria Cristina, Rio Lerma 31, col. Cuauhté-
moc, Mexico:

The door, dark wood with a diamond pattern embossment, door
knob and chain in gold metal, opens directly onto the room, a
5 x 5 meters square. The walls and ceiling, about 3 meters high,
are coated in thick white roughcast. The carpet is pale mauve
with grayish-blue speckles arranged in squares.

On the right-hand wall as you enter, just before the door to
the bathroom—which is the same model as the front door—are
posted two little signs under glass, with tiny lettering: *Instruc-
tivo de protección y seguridad para huespedes.* After the bathroom, there's the Toshiba TV set placed at a height of about 1.7
meters on top of a shelf made of red wood held in place by two
chains riveted to the wall. Beneath, a luggage rack covered in
laminate and a streamlined floor fan on a gray stand about 1.5
meters high. Next, another door, same as the last two, opens
into a closet.

The wall facing the front door has a rectangular window
measuring about 1.5 meters long and 1.2 meters high, consisting of two large panes set in a black metal frame, the right-hand
pane sliding over the other, fitted on the outside with a screen.
There are voile curtains and drapes made of a print fabric with
a kind of wavy pattern in predominantly green and light mauve.
Out the window, you can see right down to the hotel patio, tiled

in ochre and copper green, graced with a triple-tiered fountain at the center, and framed by four four-story ochre facades. All around there are clumps of greenery, a few orange trees in planters, benches. What I notice immediately opposite me is a dark silhouette in a rectangle of light: is it a woman brushing her hair in a mirror, with her back to me, or is it myself, reflected in that mirror? To the left, above the tile roof, the tip of a gray concrete building, and the gray Mexico City sky.

The bed, a double, covered with the same mint-violet fabric as the drapes, abuts the third wall. The headboard is a blond wood panel that runs the length of the wall: molded rectangles separated by fluted pilasters with a knob at each end. On either side of the bed is a night table with a single drawer, topped with the same bonded wood as the luggage rack. On the left-hand table, a touchtone phone. Above each, a wall lamp in gold metal tubing and a white fabric shade. Higher up, centered over the bed, an unattractive painting of a mountain lake.

Against the last wall—the one to the right of the front door— is a long desk with five drawers, daubed in a muddy brown and topped with a pale laminate similar to the two already described. A wooden lamp with a white canvas shade is set on the left-hand side of the desktop, over which hangs a mirror that spans its entire length—around 1.5 meters wide and 75 centimeters tall— into which I gaze at my walrus-like countenance: this time, alas, I'm sure that it's mine. Depressed at the sight, I turn back to the window and see myself, definitely me, reflected in the other mirror, symmetrical to this one: me, without a doubt, since the black silhouette—a housemaid, a sprite?—has moved off to the right. Above the mirror (mine) is a painting in a dark frame showing the courtyard of some ancient house with bougainvillea climbing around the door and a dome atop the roof. A moment later, I turn back to the window: the black silhouette is there once more, motionless in front of the mirror. It's impossible to know whether she's facing me, or, with her back to me, can see me in the mirror just the same. And suddenly the outline created there on the other side of the hotel courtyard, like a sort of chessboard pawn on its white square, evokes the memory of my own silhouette, four months ago, at the window of room 313 of the Hotel Metropole (5 Place du General de Gaulle, in Metz). Rectangle of light in the blackness of night, curtains flying, pathos.

Even leaving aside the situation I was in at that time, there was definitely something creepy about that room, which one entered directly through a lacquered cream door. From the ceiling, right above the bed, hung a light bulb enclosed in a clear plastic globe bristling with little spikes, looking quite a bit like the generic representation of a virus. The walls were papered in a beige-pink pattern of faintly embossed diamond shapes, and the short pile carpet was brown (not so much a carpet, actually, as a series of square felt panels). Along the wall on the right-hand side as you entered, there was an enormous cast-iron radiator (painted over so many times that the paint formed waves, as though it was whipped cream), topped by a cream-colored shelf. Next, a narrow mirror, measuring about 20 centimeters x 1 meter. Then, a table in pale wood, on whose glass-topped surface sat a Gründig TV, a lamp with a white shade, and a glass ashtray. In front of the table, two chairs in pale wood with seats upholstered in brown velvet with red motifs (some kind of berry?). On the right-hand portion of the wall facing the door, there was a window made up of two cream-colored PCV casements surmounted by a panel of eight fixed panes. Whitish voile curtains, not the cleanest, and a metal awning. Out the window, one could see plane trees, whipped about by the rain, along the avenue leading to the imposing Prussian train station where Jean Moulin is presumed to have died while being transferred to Germany by his captors; if you leaned out a bit, your could see the Babylonian gateway to the central hall, covered in green tile. Under the window was a luggage rack in pale wood. The bed, covered with a down comforter in royal blue with a white border, was against the third wall. The headboard and night tables were in pale wood, and above each was a wall lamp in gold metal adjustable tubing, with a white shade.

It was raining on the plane trees, on the green roof tiles of the Prussian train station, it was raining on Metz, and there I was, crying like a baby, for Mélanie Melbourne had left me. I was obsessively replaying the scene wherein she gently closed the hallway door, blowing me a last kiss from the tips of her fingers (it didn't occur to me at the time, but presently, as I lie on the mint-violet bed of room 309, recalling that awful night, what comes to mind are the last lines of *Antony and Cleopatra*); then another scene where, leaning out the window, I watched her walk away toward the train station, a frail silhouette wrapped in a cheap, close-fitting pink plastic raincoat that sparkles in the rain; or still others where I would stupidly return to the window and lean out, in hopes of seeing what? Her coming back, or her leaning against a plane tree, looking up at my window—aren't we just idiotic sometimes?—but there was nothing except the night and the rain and the leaves ripped away by the wind and the tragic shadows of the Prusso-Babylonian train station. And at present, I'm wondering whether it isn't her, Mélanie Melbourne, signaling to me from the other side of the courtyard of the Hotel Maria Cristina, from the other side of the mirror. What kind of a jam has she gotten herself into now? Who else, if not me, could get her out of it? Aren't we just idiotic sometimes . . .

Text handwritten on pages torn from Leaves of Grass, *by Walt Whitman, Aubier-Flammarion, bilingual edition.*

19

Room 117, Astor Hotel, 956 Washington Avenue, Miami Beach:

Without a doubt, one of the most discretely elegant rooms I've ever stayed in. The lacquered white door opens into a small vestibule, about 1 x 1.2 meters, whose drop ceiling conceals the air-conditioner. To the right, a frosted glass door set in a white frame opens into the bathroom, and two white shuttered doors conceal a closet.

The room itself measures about 6 x 6 meters. The walls are painted in a light *café au lait,* the ceiling, about 3 meters high, is white, and the carpet beige. The wall to the right upon entering is bare. Abutting the wall that forms a right angle with this one is the bed, covered in a dark *café-au-lait* fabric, topped with a white comforter. The headboard consists of a large panel of pale wood crimped with aluminum, at the center of which is a porthole of frosted glass also banded in aluminum, giving off a milky glow. On either side of the bed is a night table in pale wood with quadrangular legs and topped with a glass shield. Above each (the right-hand one as you face the wall has a white telephone on it) is a swivel wall lamp in tubing with a black matte metallic shade. All the lights (apart from the little desk lamp) are equipped with dimmers.

On the wall facing the entry, there's a rectangular window measuring about 2 meters wide by 1.6 meters tall, made up of two glass panes set in aluminum, broken up into three horizontal strips by two flat white plastic bars. Outside, you can see a parking lot at the foot of a small, cream-colored building, whose Venetian-blinded windows face those of the room. A wall topped by some white grillwork separates the hotel from the parking lot, where you can see, among other vehicles, a flaming red pick-up truck. A heavy, grayish-beige canvas shade folds and unfolds (like the sail of a Chinese junk) over the window. A very modern-looking desk sits in front of it: a parallelogram in pale wood with a glass-covered hole exposing the contents of the compartmented drawer beneath, and flat, girder-like legs in black matte metal. On the desk is a little lamp in brushed aluminum on a spindly stem and quadrangular base, fitted with a truncated shade in white plastic. In front of the desk, a chair composed of two slightly curved panels of pale wood, mounted on brushed aluminum legs. To the right of the window, a tall parallelepiped of an armoire in pale wood, with double doors whose handles are each a stroke of black wood.

In the corner made with the fourth and final wall, set on the diagonal, is a little table on casters. On the lower shelf is a Sony stereo system, and above it, an RCA television. Next comes a luggage rack in light wood with black straps, then a luxuriously padded armchair, upholstered in a light *café-au-lait* fabric. Above, an art photo under glass in a thin black wood frame, showing two *bricole*—the mooring posts in the Venetian lagoon. To the left of the armchair, the cube-shaped chest in pale wood that holds the minibar is set in front of the closet with the shuttered doors. On its top, a slightly concave part of which is lined in brushed aluminum, are arranged an ice bucket, two glasses, a T-shaped corkscrew, and an isothermal wine cooler in brushed aluminum containing a bottle of Dom Pérignon. And magazines—*Florida, Paper, Ocean Drive*—the latter containing photo essays on a number of frighteningly gorgeous women. Among them, there's Sonia Incarnación: a little sand sprinkled over her dark skin, a bikini that seems to be made out of a very few blue-green fluorescent butterfly wings—the wings of the tropical butterflies whose flight over the sea off Havana is scattered by the wind—and a face in tobacco leaf tones, with gently slanted mint leaf eyes beneath curved lashes. Curved, yes, her lashes—like the waves breaking on South Beach, two blocks from the hotel; and green are her eyes, yes, flecked with yellow and violet, with eyebrows as slender and long as the antennae of a golden scarab.[1] These eyes, those brows, I gaze at them, tracing them with my fingertip, then with my tongue, while Sonia, whom I prefer to call Incarnación, stretched out on her stomach on the white comforter, pages through the section of *Ocean Drive* that is about her. The incredible curves of her incarnation. In the centerfold shot, her legs are tucked to one side, flecked with sand like so many tiny mirrors, and—leaning on her left arm—she's licking an ice-cream cone (mango ice cream, she specifies), showing her round haunch, her prominent shoulder, and also her peachy little *pechos* (also prominent), that would make the Pope cry: a pair of mortal sins incarnate, around

---

1   This sentence, as well as the previous one (in blatantly poor taste) is ripped off from a famous book, guess which (*Salambô*? The *Poèmes barbares*?). *(AN)*

which my hands are cupped . . . [2] She drops the magazine, casts me a pouting look, she can't read while I'm doing that (she calls that reading), *¿y cómo me encuentras?* she asks me: how do I think she looks? *Atómica.* I know that Incarnación is going to make my life very complicated, but are simple lives worth living? I was on vacation in Coral Gables, at the Biltmore, cozying up with Arlette Harlowe, the heiress (among other things) to the Colgate toothpaste fortune, everything was going smoothly, we were starting to get pleasantly bored. And then one fine evening, while drinking a *mojito* in the lobby, underneath a bird cage, in the company of a sort of production assistant, there was this girl whose very short black dress and fluorescent green necklace kept her just this side of total nudity, which wasn't necessarily her customary state, but was obviously her natural state (I don't know if I'm making sense). And ever since (and especially ever since I noticed, on one of the marina docks, the silhouette of a flat-headed gorilla that may well have been Medusa[3]), when we leave each morning, Atómica and I, in our mauve powerboat, to go cruising down the Havana shoreline, casting our butterfly nets to collect the fluorescent specimens that the wind has blown out to sea (*las mariposas de mi terra,* she exclaims in one breath,

---

2   Ibid. *(AN)*
3   Well, maybe not Medusa, because by then I had already done him in, as I recall, at the end of a chase across the rooftops of Bucharest, but some other hired assassin—there's no shortage of them. Medusa, if I'm remembering it correctly, fell without a sound from the roof of the APA BUCURESTI, Bucharest Water, right onto the roof of a Dacia, crushing it like a top hat, killing the driver along with himself: that model of Renault made for the Eastern Bloc underclass was cheap junk, and you can sue me if I'm lying. *(AN)*

while I remove the blue-green cotton butterfly that rests on her breasts), ever since that night at the Biltmore Hotel, I can't help but wonder whether the boats silhouetted on the horizon aren't staffed by a crew of assassins hired by Arlette Harlowe.

> *Text handwritten on five postcards* ("Twilight sets in the Art Deco district of Miami Beach," "Miami Beach aerial view of Lincoln Road," "Hotel Astor," "South Beach collection: Essex House," "South Beach collection: Loews").

20

Room 102, Auberge Saint-Pierre, Mont-Saint-Michel:

The door, in pale oak with a gilt handle, leads directly into the room, which measures about 3.5 x 5.5 meters; it opens into one of the lengthwise sides, with the windows parallel. The ceiling, white, bordered with white molding, is around 3 meters high. The walls are hung in a very pale ochre fabric mottled with barely discernable white shapes, conjuring up the sickening "skins" that used to float on the warmed milk of my childhood. A baseboard of the same wood as the door runs along the bottom of the walls. A pink carpet flecked with beige evokes the rather unpleasant impression of a drunk's vomit.

The wall to the immediate right of the entrance contains the closet door, 2 meters high and 60 centimeters wide: the double panels are hung in the same fabric as the walls, and are framed in beige-painted wood. Next comes the desk, on which I have placed my computer: a simple parallelepiped whose top, a grayish rose, granite-like stone (also a bit pukey) holds a lamp with a chunky octagonal base in lacquered ivory and an oval shade of white canvas. A mirror in a frame of the same color of lacquered wood hangs above the desk. Above the lamp, almost in the corner made with the windowed wall, a small Radiola television is bracketed. In front of the desk are a stool and a bamboo chair painted in the same ivory tone, fitted pale ochre cushions webbed in red, with a four-leaf floral motif in each diamond shape. Sitting in this chair, I begin a book by Georges Perec. However long it takes, I won't leave here until I've finished it. When I say "here," mind you, I mean: Mont-Saint-Michel, not my room. I'm not that fanatical. I allow myself a few walks along the ramparts—it clears the head. I've bought myself a pair of Zeiss binoculars, which I intend to use to do some bird-watching (to this end, I have also purchased a pocket ornithological encyclopedia translated from English). Yesterday I think I sighted a flock of oystercatchers. Distinguishing an oystercatcher from a great black-backed gull is no great feat, I grant you, but I'm only a beginner. I'm sure to be much better at it by the time I've finished the book. The Perec book, I mean. I'll know how to tell the common ringed plover from the ruddy turnstone, for instance.

The wall facing the entrance contains two deep-set twin window frames about 1 meter from the floor, above a shelf cantilevered from the wall and an electric radiator. They consist of two casements with two panes each that close with a window catch, and above the cross bar, two separate transoms. The frames are in oak, like the door. Four little white lace curtains embroidered in a frieze of leaves and butterflies cover the panes. Set over the frames are drawstring drapes in sausage-colored plasticized canvas. Out the windows, you can see those of the house across the way, very close, with the restaurant "The Seagulls" on the ground floor (named for seagulls perhaps, but every windowsill is bristling with spindly little pikes clearly intended to dissuade such gulls from alighting). Above the slate roof, brightly lit, are the choir and steeple of the abbey. I chose this inn for the peace and quiet, its isolation. It's winter now, the month of January, and apart from a few bundled-up schoolchildren coming from Pontorson or Avranches, and the odd ruddy English couple, you don't see a soul on the island all day. In the evening, apart from the restaurant at the inn, and the one run by Mama Poulard (and "The Seagulls," of course, but only on weekends), everything is closed, muffled in mist, beaded in drizzle, leaving few temptations to lure me away from my book. The stillness, the exertion (climbing up to the monastery entrance is no small matter), the at-once monotonous and exhilarating sight of the tides, the healthy, balanced meals: this regimen seems to suit the goal I've set myself. Without overestimating my wherewithal, I hope to be finished in two months.

The third wall contains the door to the bathroom, much like the closet door, but wider. To the right of this door is a little three-tiered chest of drawers in braided rattan and bamboo, painted the same eburnean whitish-gray as noted above, and topped in the same vomit-colored stone as the desk. Framed in white and gilt, a thing representing shored-up fishing boats in a sort of mist or haze. Above, a sconce topped with a half cone of frosted glass with orangey streaks (forgot to say that the same is fixed to the wall between the two windows).

The bed, flanked by two night tables of the same style as the chest of drawers—but smaller, obviously, with just one drawer —abuts the same wall as the entrance. On each night table is a lamp replicating the one on the desk, but at three-quarter scale. On the right-hand table, in addition, there's an ivory telephone, Matra brand. Above the rectangular headboard, in eburnean bamboo/rattan, more hazy fishing boats. And the bedspread? Ah, the bedspread, if you must know, is predominantly puke pink (or denture pink, if you'd rather), with touches of blue and white.

So, it's my intention to write the book that Perec refers to in *Species of Spaces:* "It's no doubt because the space of the bedroom works for me like a Proustian Madeleine (. . .) that I undertook, several years ago now, to make an inventory, as exhaustive and as accurate as possible, of all the 'Places Where I Have Slept.'" Yet, as far as I know, Perec never finished the work as planned. So, I'm going to do it for him: not out of arrogance, but rather out of a kind of respect bordering (perhaps) on devotion. When it comes to the authors I love, I can't bear the idea that they left a project incomplete. So, in all modesty, I do it for them. My way of reading these works is to complete them, that's all (or to put it more precisely, to save them from incompletion). Thus, I've written endings for *Bouvard and Pécuchet, The Castle, The Trial, Dead Souls,* etc. (as for *The Man Without Qualities,* I just haven't found the energy yet). What you presently hold before your eyes is the eighth section ("Hotels") of *Places Where I Have Slept*[1] by Georges Perec (I always begin books at the end).

Text printed out, via computer.

---

1   As I had to leave the Saint-Pierre Inn after just a couple of days (I couldn't bear living among its loathsome roses any longer), I haven't been able thus far to pursue these "Hotels," much less get started on writing the other parts of the book project ("My Bedrooms," "Dormitories and Barrack-Rooms," "Friends' Bedrooms," "Houses in the Country," "Trains, Boats, etc."). But I'll get around to it one of these days. *(AN)*[2]

2   Assuming that we take this declaration of intent at face value, here is what we can reasonably infer from the (scarce) evidence in our possession: this project—to write *The Places Where I Have Slept*—was never resumed in any systematic way, according to the plan put forward here; yet, never entirely forsaken either, its eighth section ("Hotels") was regularly augmented, at the author's whim, throughout his travels. His death, which came about in the precise place and circumstances he had predicted (see the twenty-third "room"), prevented him, in the end, from concluding the undertaking (or rather, from going back to the start). This conjecture is risky, however, and leaves many questions unanswered (why, for example, were these fragments, plainly written on different dates—see the variety of supports—brought together, and by whom, into the briefcase found by Madame ***?). Besides, the fact that we have thus far come across no trace of the completed *Bouvard and Pécuchet,* of *The Castle,* nor any other of the books supposedly "finished" by the author, leaves enormous room for speculation as to the validity of his "explanations," which we, for one, are inclined to see as ploy meant to mislead the reader. We therefore publish this *Hotel Crystal* leaving unresolved the question as to whether it is indeed the final, unfinished part of what would have been a more extensive, complete, and systematic work. Whatever the case may be, if there should be readers wishing to pay to his text the same peculiar tribute that the author claimed to be paying to Georges Perec, by adding the seven missing sections, they should feel free: we grant prior authorization for them to do so, and even thank them in advance. *(EN)*

21

Room 1213, Hotel Hilton Bonaventure, 1 Place Bonaventure, Montreal:

The front door, in dark wood, opens into a hallway about 1.5 x 3 meters. The walls are papered in fine beige and white stripes printed over with vague gray shapes (filaments, wrinkled paper, cracks?). The carpet is beige sprinkled with greenish-gray dashes. To the right opens the door to the bathroom, painted in white and bearing a full-length mirror. To the left, the closet door, also white. The ceiling, about 2 meters high, consists of metal slats, with a recessed halogen light.

The room itself measures a spacious 8 x 5 meters. The carpet and walls are the same as in the hallway, but the ceiling is higher (about 3 meters), painted in white and framed by a large band, also white. To the left as you enter, in the corner made by the wall and the closet, an enormous minibar built into a red wood cabinet is topped in marble, and arranged on top are a white tray, an electric coffee maker with two cups and a couple of packets of coffee, an ice bucket, and four glasses, two of which are stemmed. Next comes the luggage rack covered in a bottle-green striped fabric, then some hideous cabinet affair in red wood, a kind of high tabernacle oddly crested with a double pitched roof, and whose doors conceal a RCA television. Then, perpendicular to the wall, beneath a mirror where I stare at my face in disbelief (my eyes seem made out of melted candle wax), a straight-legged desk in red wood, flanked by two armchairs upholstered in a fabric of green-beige-orange geometric shapes. On the desk are a white telephone and a lamp too complicated to describe,[1] in a metal that has the appearance of copper turned verdigris.

The wall facing the entrance contains, on the left-hand side, a sliding glass door, all in one piece, in a black metallic frame, with a narrow sliding pane to the right, which opens onto a kind of narrow watchtower walk strewn with pebbles. White voile curtains, then drapes in a green on beige pattern, then a second layer of drapes in green and ochre stripes, are all drawn over this plate glass door, which commands an immense view: in the middle of the tableau, dividing it into two equal parts, are the Bonaventure highway glittering with headlights, and the tracks of the central train station. In the background, beyond a building on which a red neon sign blinks "Five Roses Flour," the pale line of the Saint Lawrence Seaway, spanned by the Victoria Bridge. Further back, on the other bank, antennae and chimneys crowned with red beacons emerge out of the glow of orange light. To the left, a quadrangular fifty story high-rise, and a smaller, dihedral one crowned by a kind of glass-plated flying saucer, lit in blue from below. Elevators glide at the angle of the dihedron, one of whose wings bears white neon letters spelling DELTA. Next, moving toward the center of the tableau, a lower-lying business district descends to the river, on either side of Rue McGill. At the horizon, one glimpses a line of docks in the Old

---

1   I could do it, but . . . *(AN)*

Quarter of Montreal. To the right of the median formed by the Bonaventure train tracks, great urban expanses, orange lights, pale glass façades like water lilies, stretch in parallel along the river: Saint Antoine, Saint Jacques, Notre Dame. After the corner made with the third wall, there's an armchair upholstered in the same striped bottle-green fabric as the luggage rack, with a large, heavily padded footstool, and a floor lamp consisting of three verdigris metal columns holding a flared cup in white frosted glass.

The bed, extremely wide, abuts the third wall. The headboard, made in the same dark red wood as the TV cabinet, is vaguely "pedimented." The quilted bedspread is in the same green and ochre-striped fabric as the drapes. To the left of the bed, on a little round, four-legged table, in the same non-style as the writing desk, sit a lamp of verdigris columns supporting two fake candles topped by a white, pleated shade, as well as a second telephone. To the left of the table, on the wall, is a painting under glass attributed to a certain Calvé, representing a garden path, or some gently descending staircase, in an arboretum. A second painting by the same Calvé showing a flowery meadow next to a lake, under glass in a gilt frame, is hung on the fourth wall, which is shared on the other side by the bathroom.

Last night, I didn't sleep in the green and ochre striped bed. I didn't sleep at all, in fact: I drank until dawn in the bars along the Boulevard Saint-Laurent with Iskandar Arak-Bar, who came (or so he says—and maybe it's true, after all) to visit some family members living in exile in Montreal. When, at 7 A.M., I enter the dining room of the Hilton, I'm tolerably plastered. As I move toward the buffet, with the idea of procuring a couple of gallons of orange juice, my gaze (sidelong) is arrested forcibly by the legs of a girl in shorts just ahead of me: ankles that seem to have been crafted by a luthier—thighs, rounded calves, as sleek as fine fish (one is easily ridiculous when describing the indescribable, a woman's legs, and I'm no exception), suggesting a lively suppleness, honey-like, with just a hint of blond peach fuzz, giving off an athletic, open-air quality, I would almost say ecological, a kind of radiant naïveté that one finds only in countries fed on cornflakes and fortified milk . . . America, Australia . . . Anglo-Saxon legs, I mean. Does Protestantism also have something to do with it? I wonder, vaguely, confusedly, while my trembling hand fills a glass with orange juice. No, I don't think so. All that beauty planted in a pair of Nikes, alas. And the Nikes aren't the only thing wrong with the picture: there's also a pair of hairy legs next to her, planted in a pair of walking shoes, Rockports, with socks sagging at the ankles. Jerk. They go sit down at a round table with a garnet-colored tablecloth, sit down with their sausages, their cornflakes and their fruit juices. Then he gets up and leaves. Forgot something in their room, probably. Without so much as a second thought—absolutely lucid, determined, composed, Napoleonic—I launch my attack. My gaze meets hers, and something tells me that my boldness will be rewarded. I grab a spoon, which I drop in the vicinity of her table, then I crouch down and, in an instant, nimble as a cat, I'm under the garnet-colored tablecloth. There, curled up, my heart racing, I wait a second more, nothing happens, no screams, so I begin, very lightly, to fondle her ankles, imagined more than seen in the dimness. To shed some light, I lift a bit of tablecloth. God, what a vision! Still, the Nikes are annoying: I remove them, gently, as though from the feet of a queen. Lovely, spirited feet, tan uppers and baby pink undersides. Leaning over, I kiss them, cautiously slipping my tongue, by little strokes, as it were, between the long toes with nails painted silver. Ah! I must have gone too far, a delightful little shudder, a contraction, I must have tickled her. Raising her leg slightly, I take her toes in my mouth and nibble them. I climb slowly up the calf, caressing gently. Damn! Two hairy legs suddenly burst onto the scene. I'd practically forgotten about them, and one of his feet nearly kicked me. I don't budge for a few seconds, my heart racing, then resume my ascent. Delectable knees, two polished pebbles cupped in my hands. Now she crosses her legs, passing the right over the left, exactly as I would have wanted: is she reading my mind? Placing her right foot on my now supercharged cock, I knead her knees, I wet my index finger with saliva, slip it into the fold between her right knee and her left thigh, and slide it in and out. We're carrying on like this for a short while when she deftly uncrosses her legs, withdraws her right foot, and then, wonder of wonders . . . a silvery-nailed hand, wrist bound in a cord bracelet, holding an eyeliner pencil, reaches beneath the tablecloth and writes on her instep, in English: HIGHER! Christ! This girl's outmaneuvering even me! Granted, I took the initiative, but here I think I've met my match. Higher! High as you like, honey. She scoots her chair closer to the table. I place my hand flat on her thigh and slowly commence climbing, crawling, so to speak, up her leg. Higher, ever higher, to where it flares and tightens, opens and shuts: origin of the world, we all agree, but origin too of dialectics. Actually, I'm just saying that . . . but what business is it of mine, after all? I hear them talking up there. Going to go to Tadoussac to see the whales. Why am I not surprised . . . *So exciting* . . . Giant animals playing in the waves . . . I stick my snout between her golden thighs, mmm, something warm in the oven . . . His walking shoes are twitching nervously. Of course, Jim, go see the whales. The legs have parted, so as to facilitate my hand's journey. At this point, though, I'll have to force my way a little, gently, tight fabric, denim, patience, then a bit of something silky, then bingo! I'm into the wetness, a finger soon titillating a rather one-of-a-kind clitoris, mustn't go too far too fast, her legs tighten a little. They go there to breed, or to feed, the whales do, I'm not getting all of it through his American accent, feeding, breeding, it's Jim who's giving the lecture, he must have brought their *Lonely Planet* down from the room. With that, the fool gets up to get more sausages, no doubt, and so I take advantage of the opportunity to make my move. Honey and I are about to take it to the next level. Her legs tighten convulsively, imprisoning my hand, releasing it, tightening once again, it's all going very well when she suddenly hits my jaw with her knee, nearly knocking me out. My skull hits the table, causing the place settings to jingle, and I almost roll out from under the tablecloth on the other side. Did she do that on purpose, or accidentally, out of pleasure? And now Jimmy's back again. Time to calm down. The jerk is still talking about whales, about other places in the world where you can see them, Baja California, Patagonia. He's reciting his lesson when he suddenly seems to notice a certain distractedness in his partner (I wonder: are they married? I wasn't paying attention a moment ago when the hand slipped under the tablecloth to write "HIGHER": was there a wedding ring or not? For that matter, are wedding rings worn on the right hand? I dunno, I've never had one), distractedness, and thus, inattention: Are you listening to me, honey? And with that, he places his hand on Honey's thigh. Shit! Within an inch of mine! My heart skips a beat! Left hand (he's sitting to her right), ring finger duly ringed: married, then. On their honeymoon? That would be too much. Well, of course she's listening, she's all ears, she simpers. Yeah, right . . . The hand promptly withdraws, he's suddenly in a rush, they have to get going, it's a long drive to Tadoussac. Okay, Honey, get moving. Ah, but I've got her where I want her, now . . . I'm the one who's got her Nikes . . . She's talking with her toes, as it were, comically begging for mercy. I let her sweat as Jim gets increasingly annoyed. All right, just a second, could you get me a little more tea . . . But what about me? I'm going to make her pay for that knee to the jaw! But in the end, I sense that things are getting nasty up there, which is not really in my interest. I put her shoes back on, she gets up, *adieu* Honey, but I do hold on to one souvenir: a shoelace (the right one).

Text handwritten on the blank pages left "at the request of the author" at the end of Je me souviens, *by Georges Perec, published by Hachette in the "Librairie du XX siècle" series.*

22

Room 1123, Hotel Abşeron, Baku, Azerbaidjan:

The front door opens into a little hall, about 2.5 x 1.25 meters, entirely paneled in varnished wood, mahogany colored, suggestive of the interior of a passenger ship, or in any case, of the liner I took as a child, on the passage to Africa.[1] On the left, a five-pegged coatrack beneath a shelf, then a mirror measuring about 80 centimeters high and 20 wide. To the right opens the door to the bathroom. Ivory plastic light switches, mottled gray carpet (same as the rest of the room), and cream-colored ceiling with a spotlight that doesn't work.

The room itself measures about 6 x 4 meters, the walls are hung in an odd plastic-coated paper representing gray tree limbs, slightly embossed on a grainy white and beige background sprinkled with glitter. In the center of the ceiling, painted white, hangs a complicated chandelier with pendants, multifaceted balls and leaves (or conch shells?) of pink iridescent porcelain, rather obscene. The walls (except for the one facing the entrance, which contains the glass doors leading to the balcony) are paneled in varnished wood up to about 75 centimeters from the ceiling. To the left as you enter, there's a closet with a sliding door in varnished wood, then a chair in pale wood, the seat and back done in brown, then a little cube-shaped cabinet

---

1   During this crossing, I recall having pushed my English governess overboard. *(AN)*

in brown wood containing a few plates and place settings; on top, a circular glass tray bearing a pitcher and two glasses.

The wall facing the entrance is taken up entirely by the plate glass window composed of a door, on the left, that opens onto the balcony, and, on the right, two panes one above the other—and a cream-colored air-conditioner, model БК 2300, is wedged in the bottom one. Over the windows hang white, flowery macramé curtains and drapes in a purple woolen fabric that you could imagine as a Roman emperor's mantle. On the balcony, the low-slung railing looks hazardous for drunks. Looking straight out, on the far side of an intersection that must be the world's largest, where the militia park their vehicles, one can see a gigantic palace—call it Stalin-meets-Venice—whose slender pinnacles add a certain Tudor touch, built by an East German architect (this construction also calls to mind the towering architectural features seen in the background of certain Renaissance paintings). In the distance, the Abşeron peninsula glistens in the night, surmounted by two very tall antennae studded with red lights. To the left, past a spacious boulevard and a promenade where unpretentious merry-go-rounds are spinning, the Caspian Sea shines in the moonlight, slashed by the black lines of two long jetties. Boats at their moorings are all aglow. To the right, the city, beneath skeins of yellowish clouds.

The bed, broad and low to the ground, abuts the third wall. It's covered by a bedspread in an ugly, multicolor geometric pattern, dominated by yellows and pinks. Hanging on the wall above, a poor-quality color print like the ones you see in the

Third World representing a meadow at a bend in a river, trees turning autumnal. To the right of the bed, two armchairs in garnet plush are arranged around a table skirted in purple, holding an olive-green rotary telephone and an ashtray. To the right of the armchairs, in the corner where the wall meets the bathroom partition, is a rather sizable, dirty-looking and broken Cinar brand refrigerator. A bouquet of plastic flowers—faded daisies and red roses—has been placed on top. Against the bathroom wall, a cube-shaped, three-drawer chest bears a РЕКОРД brand television.

This is the room where I used to hang out, back when I was dabbling in smuggled caviar with Mourad Mamardachvili and Themistocles Papadiamantides; and this is the room where I will die. The matter has been decided. Where better to end up than in a hotel whose name is (almost) that of the great river of the underworld? I'll gaze into the mirror at the entrance and contemplate the handiwork of Time: wattle-like jowls will adorn my cheeks, my eyes (that, back in the day, women once compared to those of a tiger) will have started to bulge, their luster now faded; my Cyrano-nose will be shot through with a network of scarlet veins, and be sprouting gray hairs, as will my ears; the skin on my skull will show through my thinning hair, like sand beneath algae. All my features fallen, the inevitable pear-shaping set it. The work of gravity (helped along by substantial amounts of alcohol). Old pelican-face. Here's how it will go. I'll walk out onto the balcony, I'll watch from a distance, from above, the young, dark-haired women as they stroll two by two along the glittering seashore, sucking at ice-cream cones, casting sidelong glances at bands of mustachioed young men. I'll recall the night from the bygone past when, in the steeply sloped streets of the old city, I stalked and approached the serpentine form of Pashmina Pachelbel, queen of the Turks (as astounding as it may seem, even—presently—to myself, we made love seven times that night, before the muezzin had issued the call to dawn prayers). At present, I'll muse, wheezing under a layer of lard, Pashmina is living out her last inglorious days in London, as an aging, two-bit madam. I'll gaze out at the illuminated ships at anchor, recalling the time when, in the cool evening air, I would be rowed out for a glass of ouzo aboard Themistocles's cargo boat (and the next day, we would cast off, dead drunk, for the Volga delta where our fishermen awaited us, and once we'd taken on as much beluga sturgeon eggs as we could hold, there among the low-lying islands, we partied like a couple of Cossacks in the dives of Astrakhan; and one night, with reference to a rendition of Tchaikovsky's sextet *Souvenir de Florence,* we got into an animated discussion with some Soviet tank drivers—it was on this occasion that we made the acquaintance of Ilyuchinsk, a comrade who's better to have as a friend than a foe: by the end of our little controversy, Themistocles had to go in for a new set of chrome-plated dentures). I'll recall the time we smuggled out the blueprints of the Proton rocket engines in a can of caviar . . . but that's another story, which I'll tell when the time comes (maybe). I'll have one last look at the city beneath tattered mauve clouds, the glimmering pincer of the Abşeron Peninsula, the Caspian in the moonlight, the insane palace, and then I'll go back into my room. Sitting on one of the garnet plush armchairs, I'll write a letter to Mélanie Melbourne. I'll seal it, and then, when I go to write the address on the envelope, I'll realize that I no longer know where in the world she might be living. I'll write a second letter, then, to the attention of the Consul General of France, requesting that he not go to the needless expense of repatriating my corpse, that he should give it to Azeri science instead, which needs everything it can get, and that he devote the unspent funds to tracking down a certain Melbourne, Mélanie, French citizen (though also British and Australian), so as to forward the enclosed letter to her. This, Consul General, sir, I will add, represents my most cherished last will: execute it as stated, or live with a curse upon your head. Then I'll put a cassette into the little player, madrigals by Gesualdo. I'll draw from my bag a 9MM Makarov pistol, sold to me at three times the going price by Mehmet Mamardachvili, Mourad's son: a heavy, cunning young man, treacherous to the bone, a rare specimen. It's all over, I'll think to myself—even the crooks aren't what their fathers used to be. It's definitely time to be done with it.

> *Text handwritten on three sheets of hotel stationary, "Hotel Ritz /15 Place Vendôme, Paris."*

23

Room 35, The Emperor's Inn, Place Marx-Dormoy, Montélimar:

Here at least I thought I was going to get some peace and quiet. But no . . . Not even here.

The front door opens into a little vestibule that a semicircular inner window and three steps down separate from the room proper, and which measures about 3 x 1.5 meters. The pale orange carpet is printed with pale yellow crescents, and like the rest of the room, the walls are done, up to a height of about 2.5 meters, in a pale orange striped paper. Above, the walls and ceiling are painted white, as are the door frames, baseboards, and the front door. To the left of this vestibule is a bench/luggage rack upholstered in the same yellow-patterned orange carpet. Above, in thin, gold-painted wooden frames, are two paintings on silk signed Ogier—one representing a house in a clearing, the other a pond with a little bridge. To the left of the arch on the way into the room stands a wooden coatrack. To the right is the bathroom. A little white globe light fixture hangs from the ceiling.

The room itself measures about 4.5 x 6.5 meters, with the ceiling at about 3.5 meters. Along the left-hand wall, there's a collapsible luggage rack made out of wood and straps, then a rustic wardrobe with two doors and two drawers, and a high-backed, straw-bottomed chair in wood with a green seat cushion, set in front of a white door, sealed off, communicating with the room next door.

The wall facing the entrance has two tall windows: two casements with four square panes, protected by two wooden shutters, whose green paint is almost completely peeled off. Beneath each window, concealed behind sheer white curtains and rubberized cloth drapes in a blue and orange pattern on a light orange background is a whitewashed, cast-iron radiator. Between the two windows, a table in pale wood—legs slightly curved and a plate-glass top—holds an ashtray and the (inevitable) box of nougats. On the wall above, a mirror in a wooden frame with its own little cornice shelf, measuring about 75 x 50 centimeters, is flanked by two milky glass half-moon wall sconces. Two chairs with threadbare, green velvet cushions frame the table. Out the window, you can see a courtyard sprinkled with white gravel, parked cars, and a row of plane trees, their leaves a grapey green; beyond the tile-topped gate, to the right, there's a small, five-story building painted in cream and orange (fashionable colors in Montélimar, apparently). On either side of the gate, stone eagles recall that Napoleon once passed through here on his calamitous descent to the isle of Elba. To the right of the right-hand window, a minibar in light wood supports a small Philips TV.

In the third wall, to the right, is a sealed-up door, on which hangs an etching representing the chateau d'Azay-le-Rideau. Two frosted glass transoms at the top of the fourth wall look onto the bathroom. Two half-moon sconces and a couple of night tables frame the brass bed. The bedspread is cut in the same blue and orange fabric as the curtains. From the ceiling, suspended on three little chains, a frosted glass disk softens the glare of its light bulb.

What's odd is that I don't remember the kind of telephone that was in the room, nor where it was located. It must have been near the bed, since I can still picture myself, reflected in the mirror, as I answered the first call that came in that night: naked, noting to my chagrin that my waist is growing deplorably thick, and so while I'm talking I suck in my stomach and comically pump out my thorax and biceps, posing full frontal or at three quarters, positions where the thickening is less noticeable. If I'm standing in the nude, then I must have just got out of bed, and if I got out of bed, that means the phone isn't within reach—that much seems indisputable. It must be on the table with the curved legs, where the ashtray and nougat box are. It's the explosive-fake-nougat trade (yet another of Pavel Schmelk's ingenious devices) that's brought me here, but no matter, that's another story, which I'll tell when the time comes (if I'm in a good mood). I'd just got into the brass bed, and was reading chapter twenty of book twenty-two of *The Memoirs of Chateaubriand,* a commentary on "Napoleon's itinerary on the way to the isle of Elba": "The hero, reduced to disguises and to tears, weeping in his postman's jacket, in the backroom of a country inn! Was it thus that Marius stood amidst the ruins of Carthage, that Hannibal died in Bithynia, Caesar . . ." Rrrrrring . . . rrrring . . . The telephone, at this hour (one in the morning)? Could it be Schmelk? Or Mélanie Melbourne, calling for help? I jump out of bed, buck naked, and pick up the receiver, wherever it's located. "Room 35? You have Mr. Gripanng on the line," dashes off a sleepy voice with a strong southern French accent. Shit! It's (I suddenly get it) Alan Greenspan, president of the Federal Reserve. For the third week in a row, Wall Street has just closed at a near-record low, and he's all flustered, wanting to know if I'm in favor of a hike or a cut in interest rates. Basically I don't give a damn, I say, as I contemplate myself gloomily in the mirror. Raise them 1.5%, and see what happens. What a pain in the ass . . . I can't believe it . . . I get back under the covers, and go back to my *Memoirs.* True to his love-hate relationship with Bonaparte, Chateaubriand doesn't call into question the insulting account written by the Prussian Count of Waldburg, who reports various acts of cowardice on the part of the former "conqueror of the world" when he was faced with popular expressions of hatred from the royalist throngs. He does a first sketch here of the portrait (which he will fill out in book twenty-four) of the only rival he acknowledges: "Changing ethics and costumes at will, as perfect in comedy as in tragedy, this performer looks as natural in the slave's tunic as he does in king's mantle, in the role of Attalus or in . . ." Rrrring . . . rrring Jesus! They're not going to leave me alone, are they? I'm tempted not to answer, but what if it's Mélanie Melbourne? I leap out of bed, pick up the phone, and the groggy voice with the heavy nougat accent announces "Monsieur Jeinng-Clode Tricheur." Oh, Jean-Claude Trichet, okay, put him through. He sounds like he's on the verge of tears. All these big bankers are big babies, really. The French and German deficits have risen above 4%, what to do? Call for sanctions? Scrap the stability pact like an old rag? But what about the balance of trade . . . the fundamentals . . . Increase the GDP, I tell him. Sorry? He doesn't seem to get what I'm saying. Increase the GDP, I repeat, in a louder tone of voice—what are you, deaf? Uh, no, but . . . well, what I mean is, of course, that was in fact what I was thinking too, but . . . by how much, if I might ask? Look, I don't know, you've got your econometrics folks on it, don't you? Let's say, a little boost of 3%. At the very most. And now, would you mind not disturbing me again tonight? Okay? Geez. I hang up. I look at myself in the mirror, gloomily. Love handles. I get back in bed. You have to wonder what Chateaubriand would have done without Napoleon. If all he had to spill ink over was Louis XVIII, let's say. "While Bonaparte, known the world over, was fleeing France amid a chorus of curses, Louis XVIII, forgotten in most quarters, was leaving London beneath a canopy of white banners and crowns." Vice arm-in-arm with crime, the "diabolical sight" of Talleyrand and Fouché, was that next? No, of course not, that bit comes after the Hundred Days. The flight of the king, the old Prince of Condé, not knowing "whether he would be stopping at Rocroi to wage battle or whether he would be going to dine at the Grand Cerf," the echo of cannon fire at Waterloo in a hop field: the apex of the *Mémoires,* from the French Tacitus, (and something of a Proust as well, from *Time Regained*). "Silent and alone, witnessing only by ear the formidable reversal of fate, I would have been less . . ." Rrrring . . . rrrring. God almighty! This is really too much! Will I ever be able to read in peace? Is this going to go on all night? asks the increasingly uncivil and sleepy voiced night attendant. Anyway, here's Monsieur Cholera. I might have guessed: Horst Köhler, president of the IMF. The

jerk wants to know whether he should force Argentina to deval-
ue its currency, and by how much. Listen, it should be perfectly
obvious. 50% at least. Let's say 75% and leave it at that. And now,
would it be asking too much of you to stop disturbing me over
these trifles? And I slam the phone down. In the mirror, I try to
assume a Johnny Weissmuller pose. I call down to the reception
desk. If one of those jackasses calls again, tell them I'm sleeping,
but that my instructions are strict: peg the dollar to the ruble. To
the what? To the ruble, repeat after me. To the rubble, eh, ruble.
That's it, great. There'll be a little something in it for you. No, not
for them, I said, for you. Okay, good night. I do what any man
in my situation would do: in the mirror, I pensively scratch my
balls. *And so to bed,* as Samuel Pepys would say. Book twenty-
four, chapter five: "At the moment Bonaparte is leaving Europe,
abandoning his life to go forth in search of the destinies of his
death, it behooves us to examine the double life of this man . . ."
Aaaaah . . . The world can do without me very well tonight.

> *Text handwritten on four pages of graph paper torn from
> a school notebook.*

24

Room 417, Cecil Hotel, Saad Zaghloul Square, Alexandria:

It so happened that Mélanie Melbourne, on a childish whim, knowing full well that I had absolutely no memory of it, asked me to describe Room 211 of the Hotel Crystal in Nancy for her. But try as I might, I could not, even to make her happy—and making her happy was my most constant concern: nothing came to mind. She insisted: not a single detail? Your reflection in the mirror, for instance? No. Besides, that would be presuming that the room had a mirror, but I can't even be certain of that. It was already something of a feat that I could even remember the address—Rue Chanzy, number five (or maybe fifteen, or twenty-five, or fifty: in any case, five was involved)—and that I had managed to bring her back the box of macaroons, the Macaron Sisters macaroons, that had been sitting on the table. Ah, so you remember the table, don't you! No, no, I retorted (somewhat exasperated): I'm just assuming there was one, that's all; I don't think I've ever seen a hotel room (even in Siberia) without some form of table, in which case, the box of macaroons that I brought you must logically have been placed there. *Logically,* she mocked. I can't imagine what logic has to do with it . . . Then, changing her line of attack: besides, you never did give me that box, do you hear me? NEVER! To somebody else, maybe, but not to me. No, I replied (exhausted), that's impossible. What might have happened is that I ended up leaving the box in the room, or that there was never any such box in the first place. But if there was one, and if I did bring it, then you're necessarily the one I gave it to. I'd love to know what's with this "necessarily," she replied. And on it went, until the inevitable outbreak of tears.

Thus, Room 211 of the Hotel Crystal had become the empty center of our impossible life together. The last crisis, I remember it perfectly, took place in Alexandria. We were staying in room 417 of the Cecil Hotel. Mélanie Melbourne had insisted that I bring her to Alexandria, and that we stay at the Cecil, because she was completely wrapped up in reading Durrell's *Quartet* in those days. And she had developed the quirky habit—a poetic one that proved costly in the end—of reading works only in the places where they were set: Proust's *Jeunes filles en fleur* at the Grand Hotel of Cabourg, Larbaud's *Journal intime de A. O. Barnabooth* between the Florence Carlton and the Saint Petersburg Evropeiskaïa, Conrad in the Singapore Raffles, etc. Mélanie Melbourne was the love of my life, but I think she was a bit loony. Anyway, on that day, stretched out on the king-size bed with its purple and gold crisscross pattern slipcover, she was reading *Justine*. Above the dark wood headboard, a lithograph issued by the Lemercier printers in Paris, credited to a certain Alex Bida (who had also drawn a *Tarabouqa Player* that hung to the right of the window), represented a *Lady of Cairo* gazing at herself in a mirror, and what was uncanny is that this Cairo beauty resembled the reader stretched out on the bed below, in a black silk slip, legs tucked in, leaning on her forearm—one hand on her cheek, stretching her mouth and eye toward their corners, the other hand holding her book open. I don't know what suddenly gave her the notion—which, as I said, gripped her periodically—to harass me about my room in the Hotel Crystal; maybe she chanced upon the word "macaroon" in *Justine*, though this seems unlikely (I've mostly forgotten that book, in which I'd think there would be a better chance of coming across the word "Maronite," which could also have set off her train of thought).

I may have forgotten everything about the room in Nancy, but I do recall every slightest detail of the one in Alexandria. It was a vast, pretentious room, with a very high ceiling. The walls were washed in a pale yellow, the doors painted pearl gray on battleship gray, and the ceiling white; a rather impressive chandelier, trimmed with candle-holders and dripping with translucent and golden pendants, hung down from its center. The thickly piled carpet had lines of purple leaves crossing at right angles to form beige squares flecked with large purple dots. The left-hand wall as you entered the room contained a sealed-up door that once connected to another room, against which was placed a low table in dark wood that served as a luggage rack. Next came a sizable minibar paneled in dark wood, on which was perched a Goldstar TV; and then, before the hulking three-door wardrobe made of the same nearly black wood, a desk, on whose glass-covered tabletop sat a lamp with a white shade and gold metallic stand that bore a certain resemblance to a cup-and-ball game. On the wall above this hung a tallish mirror in a dark wood frame and topped with a notched pediment, and while Mélanie Melbourne, now sitting on the bed behind me, was getting mired in increasingly far-fetched suppositions—suppositions that I knew would inexorably result in a crying jag (even though they were not just a preparatory ritual leading to tears), I stared at a tanned but weary face, dark circles under its eyes, a blotchy, red proboscis, hair a greasy gray: this wizened soldier, who must not have owned any shares in mineral water, was me.

How, she asked disingenuously, can you stand there and claim to remember nothing? You can't think of something, or remember it, when it's really "nothing"—that's a contradiction. That's just the way language works, I ventured. In fact, I do remember something: the macaroons. But you said it was possible that they never existed, she countered. You should have been a teacher in a sophist school, here in Alexandria, twenty centuries ago, I said, getting up from my place in front of the mirror. Throwing open the heavy purple and gold striped draperies, I opened up the French windows and went out onto the dusty little balcony, where were jammed a white plastic chair and an enormous Carrier air-conditioner. Across the street, at the end of which one could see the corniche and the sea, partly obscured by the Qaitbey Citadel, laundry was drying on the balconies of a cramped, colorful apartment building, built in a roughly neo-Florentine style. At the time when Mélanie would have been holding forth at her school of sophistry, I would have been able to see the Pharos, the Lighthouse of Alexandria from here. You can't always think clever things, especially when being bombarded with questions that really don't call for answers.

My feigned indifference, but most especially the series of conjectures Mélanie had set in motion, and which she realized full well were impossible to resolve, were soon to bring the crisis to a head: a little trembling at first, a stifled sob in her voice, and then at last the opening of the floodgates. Mélanie wept with the absolute conviction of a little girl. I was moved by the sight, and closing the windows and solemnly drawing the curtains, I approached the bed and took her into my arms, drinking with delight the salty droplets that streamed down to the charmingly curved angles made by her lips, so inappropriately called the "corners" of the mouth. And soon after, we were making love. Owing to a sadistic inclination of mine, I happen to enjoy making love to women in tears, but this time, I can assert that I did nothing to provoke it, or not intentionally, and that my cruel fantasies were mixed, in fact, with feelings of brotherly love. Yes, I fantasized that, like some Ptolemaic king, I was fondly copulating with my tearful sister. Or, perhaps (who's to say?), my daughter.

Text handwritten on three sheets of stationary from the "Ambassade Hotel / Herrengracht / Amsterdam."

25

Room 1212, Hotel d'Angleterre, 11 Place du Port, Lausanne:

The front door opens directly into the room, whose walls are papered in cream parchment. The ceiling, white, is about 2.5 meters high, and on the beige carpet there's a mainly wine-toned throw rug measuring easily 6 x 4 meters. To the immediate left as you enter, there's an enormous, ten-element cast-iron radiator; along the same wall, a luggage rack in gold metal tubing and black straps, and finally the door to the bathroom, lacquered in cream-color.

The wall then makes a right angle toward the left. Beneath an eight-paned window in frosted glass that looks onto the bathroom, a Louis XVI secretary in a light wood that might be from a lemon tree, with coffee-and-cream leather edged in little gold studs, and a Louis XVI wing chair upholstered in a light red fabric, are all illuminated by a floor lamp formed by two brass stems supporting a truncated shade in light red fabric.

Then, the wall makes another right angle, toward the right this time, before rounding into a half rotunda containing three windows. Each one, comprised of two casements of three panes each, opens at about 1 meter high within a slight embrasure: the English-style curtains provide a screen on the inside, with blue-green-pink colored birds, flowers, and foliage on a grayish-beige background, while on the outside, hunter-green shutters slide on adjustable rails. Looking out the window, you can see: first, to the left, the Beau Rivage Hotel, bedecked with large banners; then, straight ahead, behind some stone balusters, on the grass-covered terrace (where some bronze donkeys gallivant), the central rotunda of that palace where a few barmen still reminisce wistfully about the largesse of Mobutu Sese Seko, President of Zaire; and finally, to the right: foliage, plane trees, pines and cedars, Ouchy Wharf, the lake crisscrossed by ducks, sailboats, and paddle steamers, beneath the snow-capped heights of the French shore.

Before you reach the first window, where the rotunda begins, there's a minibar with a Philips TV sitting on top. Under the central window, a sofa upholstered in bottle-green velvet is flanked by two glass-topped tables in gold metallic frames, each bearing a chunky, coffee-and-cream porcelain lamp with a truncated grayish-beige shade. In front of the sofa is a table of roughly the same make as the others, but much larger; a spidery chandelier with six somewhat unsettling gold metallic branches hangs from above, and flanking it are two armchairs upholstered in a mottled, watery green fabric. On either side of the central window are two entomological plates in thin, gilded wooden frames.

The twin beds abut the wall that extends from the rotunda. Bedspreads and headboards are done in the same fabric as the curtains: birds, flowers, foliage in blue-green-pink. Two more entomological plates hang above. On either side, on each of two little single-drawer night tables in imitation Louis XVI, is a gold metallic-stemmed lamp with a white shade. On the right-hand table is a telephone, which happens to be ringing, to let me know that my clients are waiting for me in the lobby. I reluctantly put down the book I'm reading (*Tuiles détachees,* by Jean-Christophe Bailly), check myself out in the bathroom mirror to make sure my appearance corresponds to my clients' idea (which they learned from me) of what an intellectual should look like: wild, Beethoven-like hair, a two-day beard, a black crewneck T-shirt and jacket. I brush my teeth (a compulsion of mine), grab my notes and head down to the lobby. They're all there, one reading the *Financial Times,* another *Le Figaro,* and still another *Voici Magazine:* Simplon from Bulgaria, Zig from Albania, Lampion from the land of the Tartars, Nicholas III of Russia, Dom Manuel of Brazil, and two or three others whose names escape me. In a crackling of aging joints, they extract themselves from their armchairs upon my arrival. Overall, they're in double-breasted suits, a bit frayed, V-neck sweaters, pure cashmere (a cigarette hole in Simplon's), neckties where a spot of sauce has been wont to land, and silk handkerchiefs. The emperor of Brazil is wearing two-tone shoes, the czar of Russia sports a navy-blue blazer with brass buttons over a burgundy vest, a ballpoint pen sticking out of his breast pocket—not a very classy type, according to Pashmina Pachelbel, who insisted on meeting him in order to recover (or so she maintains) some fictitious family property believed to have been stolen during some Russo-Turkish war. As if she had a family . . . Lampion is looking silly in a slightly undersized Tyrolean hat perched on the back of his head. Not much hair between the three, but a nice pair of sideburns (Nicholas III), a full beard (Zig), and a white moustache stained yellow with tobacco (Simplon).

It was Crook who came up with the idea of a school for fallen monarchs. When it comes to kings in exile, there are only two kinds: those who do nothing but gamble and marry actresses (these are the younger ones, mainly), and your dyed-in-the-wool majesties, your hardened highnesses, your recidivists who refuse to die until they've had one last fart on their throne. These are the ones, according to Crook's analysis—which seems plausible enough—who are ready to do just about anything. Vainglorious though they may be, they realize that all the skills they've acquired in this world just about qualify them for a position as chief manservant in a grand hotel. Their responses on the application forms we have them fill out are pathetic. Asked to enumerate any "special skills," they reply with things like "wild game hunting" or "dancing the foxtrot." One of them, I think it was Zig, wrote "crossword puzzles." Not one of them even knew how to play decent piano. Whence the bright idea for a crash course in The Modern World—astronomically expensive, I hardly need mention: the old codgers would spend their entire fortunes, sell their last chateaus to pay for the course, believing that restoration comes at such a price. Crook handles the subjects in Economics, and I take care of "general culture." A modern monarch, we explained to them, should be able to hold his own on a cultural television program. Our work is cut out for us.

We set up in a small sitting room the hotel has provided for us. All the offenses our pupils have endured, the pattern of their impotence, all the pains they've taken to defend their family names at any cost—these have left a residue, like the limey rings on a dirty bathroom sink, on their venerable heads—successive layers of humility, pride, and cunning. As always, they bicker over who will occupy the seat closest to mine. Lampion comes out on top. They open their notebooks, uncap their fountain pens (Nicholas III, more modern, clicks his ballpoint)—Simplon, who has a Mont Blanc, gets ink stains all over his fingers, which causes him to swear in Bulgarian. Today, I announce, once things have settled down, today I'll be talking about one of the great twentieth-century French-language writers, an unclassifiable poet, born in Belgium: Henri Michaux. Well, I'm personally acquainted with the King of Belgium, interrupts Lampion, with the inane look of a school kid showing off a T-shirt he had signed by some reality TV star. I reply curtly that one doesn't say "The King of Belgium," but rather "The King of the Belgians." An irrelevant distinction, replies the old fool. I'll have you know that revolutions took place over just such distinctions, I retort. Rrrevvv . . . ? Over *that?* Well, I'll be . . . This leaves them struck dumb. The text I've chosen for you today, I continue, unflappable, is entitled *My King.* Ah . . . They jot down the title in their notebooks. Something lively in their pen strokes, jolly in their wizened countenances, suggests that they believe revenge is theirs. I begin reading: "In the privacy of my little room, I fart in the face of my King." Long faces . . .

Text handwritten on three sheets of stationary from the "Red Roof Inn / 162 East Ontario / Chicago."

26

Room 817, Double Tree Hotel, 101 South Adams Street, Tallahassee, Florida:

The door to room 817, painted cream and equipped with a "Doorman"[1] and guard chain, opens into a vestibule of about 3 x 1.5 meters, separated from the room itself by an open half-height partition with, oddly enough, a built-in shell-shaped sink made of purple-veined stone. The carpet is gray, the walls done in coffee-and-cream wallpaper. The room itself is spacious (about 7 x 6 meters), the white roughcast ceiling is about 3 meters high. To the left of the entry, in the vestibule, two mirrored sliding doors conceal the closet, which is at a right angle to the bathroom door.

Along the right-hand wall on entering, after a sealed-off door, are two folding luggage racks in chrome tubing and black straps, then a long chest of drawers in red wood comprised of six drawers, atop which are arranged a black Sunbeam coffeemaker, a jar containing packets of decaffeinated coffee and granulated sugar substitute, two brown porcelain cups, two glasses, and a little cylindrical ice bucket. A mirror, about 1 meter high and 75 centimeters wide, in a silver metal frame, hangs above. In it, at a slight angle, I can see the bald and mustachioed head of Pavel Schmelk, his skull shining, as does a gold tooth and the circular lenses of his glasses onto which the moving images of a football

---

1   See "room" 32, note 1.

game are reflected—the local team, the Seminoles—versus the Miami Hurricanes, playing on the Panasonic television set that sits on a double-topped sideboard of red wood. That's what is on, for the moment, but just wait . . . at 21 hours 7 minutes precisely (UT), if all goes well, well, we'll see what we'll see. I keep an eye on the second hand of my Swiss Army watch.

The wall facing the entrance is taken up entirely by a bay window made up of three fixed panes set in a black metal frame. A sticker on one of them states: *Door unable to be opened by Fire Marshal.* White sheers and drapes in a floral pattern of blue, pale green, white, and ochre run the full length. From the window, you can see: to the left, a building striped horizontally in mauve, right above a rooftop parking lot and a swimming pool surrounded by lounge chairs and white outdoor tables; to the right, Adams Street (or Monroe?), where a brick church with a white steeple is topped by a green spire. Vehicles (pickup trucks, SUVs, etc.) are parked along this street, which, fifty meters further down, intersects College Avenue, lined with two-story brick buildings surrounded by sidewalks. At the end of this street (Monroe or Adams), at a short distance, rises the modern Capitol: a surbased cupola, slender columns, flanked on the left by the old Capitol, on whose bell tower both the American and Confederate flags are flying. A huge twenty-story building rises behind the new Capitol, part of the same complex. Another building, fairly tall, on the right—all beveled, furtive angles—is, along with the bell tower of the Old Capitol, the office building of the new one, and the spire, the only edifice to break up the skyline. In front of the window is a rather attractive desk in dark wood with clean lines. On it, a lamp with a square, brushed metal stand, black stem, and white skirted shade, as well as a white telephone and a little sign reading, *For your comfort, this room has been designated as non-smoking,* make up the usual furnishings. This is where Schmelk and I set up, next to the laptop, an umbrella antenna that looks exactly like one of those reflectors used by photographers. In front of the desk is a chair upholstered in black and gold checks.

The bed, enormous, covered by a bedspread in broad, mottled yellow and green stripes, abuts the third wall. The slightly curvilinear headboard is done in the same black and gold fabric as the chair in front of the desk. On either side, a single-drawer night table, made to match the chest of drawers. The one on the right when you face the wall has a large lamp with a white skirted shade and a telephone. Above the left-hand one is an articulated wall lamp in aluminum tubing with another white skirted shade.

On the last wall, which opens at one end, over the sink, is a picture in a glass and silver metallic frame. You can just make out some stairs in the middle of an ultramarine patch, surrounded by ochre motifs. It's entitled *Hittite Stairs,* and, after all, why not? In any case, that's not my problem, because in two minutes, it's going to be 21h 7mn (UT). Now it's 21h 6mn 55 sec, now 56, 57, 58, 59, 21h 7mn, blast off! The lander must have separated from the orbiter and started its descent onto the Martian atmosphere by now. Pavel Schmelk, a bit restless (you'd be restless over much less!), starts clicking away at the remote: the Seminoles-Hurricanes game disappears into the blackness, with all those helmeted hulks, and after a few moments of screen snow, then a couple of jerky images of cosmic blackness where the orbiting craft moves away looking like a golden-winged firefly, a grainy, reddish spot eats away at the bottom of the screen: we've made it! We're on our way to Mars! I take the champagne out of the ice bucket, pop the cork, and we drink a toast. The occasion certainly warrants it! Schmelk has designed an incredibly ingenious device which, by using only a laptop computer, an ordinary TV set, and an umbrella antenna, makes it possible to pirate transmissions from the Deep Space Network and thereby take control of the Mars Polar Lander probe. So while we're drinking champagne in front of a lumpy (crumbly, actually), brick-colored horizon, striped with what look like long filaments, on the other side of the continent, in Pasadena, the technicians at the Jet Propulsion Laboratory are watching, live, on their giant control screens, the Seminoles-Hurricanes game. The reddish horizon is rushing towards us. We feel like we're diving into a giant omelet that's been sprinkled a bit too liberally with paprika. Tapping away at the remote, Pavel Schmelk steers the probe with skill ("No more complicated than driving a cruise missile," he exclaims, incredulous). The spectacle is breathtakingly beautiful.[2] In the distance, a volcano

---

2 Oh, how relaxing it is to let yourself be guided, like a blind man by his dog, by a tired, old chestnut of a sentence. What a comfort! You can write like that in your sleep—it's what you might call writing (and reading, all the more so!) in business class. *(AN)*

spews a fiery geyser into the black sky. Schmelk triggers a little blast from the hydrazine engine, and off we go to the left, then straight ahead, with the towering walls of the Valles Marineris canyon opening before us, where we then dive in; Colorado, by comparison, is a cardboard backdrop for an electric train set. We meander, skid, slalom, swerve, fly between enormous cliffs so close together that we nearly get stuck, but which then open up onto great cracked plains that look like dried up swampland. We fly over landslides, over vitreous volcanic plateaus, some smooth as chocolate bars, others pocked with huge bubbles, forests of spikes, squashed pyramids . . . Ah! we chorus, a cry of admiration, for here at the end of a landscape that looks like it's carpeted in sulfur crystals we see a surging, pitch-black sea. Great waterspouts blossom into evil funnels.[3] When you think there used to be people who doubted the existence of water on Mars! But in his excitement, alas, Schmelk now makes a false move, confusing the + and − signs of the volume control on the remote (the altitude controls), and the Mars Polar Lander suddenly plunges into the inky waters, and sinks. What's worse, I was so enthralled by the sight on screen that I forgot to press "record" on the VCR. Shit!

Okay. Back down to earth. I also forgot to mention, to the left of the window, an enormous Carrier heater/air-conditioner. Between the window and the bed, beneath a floor lamp, there's a chair upholstered in coffee-and-cream fabric in wavy shapes with a matching hassock; also, hung on the wall, slightly to the

---

3   Hum . . . *(AN)*

left of the TV, there's a color photo of seashells (whorls, coils, scrolls) in a frame made of glass and black wood; finally, in the window/wall corner, an artificial ficus in a wicker planter.

Text handwritten on three sheets of paper with no letterhead.

27

Room 333, Runken Hotell, Longyearbyen, Svalbard:

The door made of pale wood opens into a little entrance hall, measuring about 1.5 x 3.5 meters, with an elephant-gray Formica floor and walls painted in oxblood red, like all the walls in this room. The left-hand wall is taken up by the closet's sliding walls, in red wood, one of whose panels holds a full-length mirror. On the ceiling above is a light fixture consisting of a single flat circle of glass.

The floor of the room proper, which measures about 4 x 5 meters, is done in the same material as the entrance hall, but in light beige. The walls, as I said, are oxblood red and the ceiling white. A frosted globe light fixture in the center. To the right as you enter, there's a Sony television on a low table. Next comes a light wood desk surmounted by a rectangular mirror, hung sideways and framed in pale wood, and then the pale wood door, trimmed in white, of the bathroom.

On the left side of the far wall is a window with four large panes, in front of which are sliding curtains in gold and purple vertical stripes printed with little suns. A flat radiator, white, sits below. The outdoor thermometer reads -10° C. Out the window you can see a snowy slope with the rock showing underneath, bearing the traces of footsteps and snowmobiles, a few telegraph poles, and blue sky at the top of the mountain.

A bentwood chair, upholstered in red, is set beneath the window. The single bed, white, abuts the left-hand wall as you enter. Above a little nightstand in pale wood is a white wall lamp. Above the bed is a picture reproducing old envelopes addressed to Svalbard, which is another name for Spitsbergen.

In this hotel, so pleasant that I'd like to come back some day with Mélanie Melbourne (though I already suspect that this, alas, is not meant to be), I'm having secret meetings with Ilyuchinsk, making preparations for the seceding of Chukotka, the immense Siberian territory bordered to the north by the Chukchi Sea, to the east by the Bering Sea, to the south by the Kamchatka Peninsula, and to the west . . . I can't quite remember now. The Yakutia, also called the Republic of Sakha, perhaps? Anyway, the only thing that matters about the region is that it's totally inhospitable—a frozen wasteland, populated only by some seventy thousand poor wretches, that its capital is called Anadyr, a name that conjures up (and rightly so) an earthly nadir—that on the other side of the Bering Strait is Alaska, and, finally and most importantly, that its subsoil is very rich in frozen mammoths and diamonds. The mammoths only interest a few romantics (forget them) but the diamonds are another story. In Chukotka, the ground is thick with them (well, you do have to dig a little, and permafrost is a little hard on the fingernails, but). So I've been commissioned by the XXXXXXXX[1] mining company to stir up a secession from the Russian Federation in this far-flung republic. Payment in diamonds, payment in kind. I'm imagining

---

1   Scratched out, illegible. *(EN)*

the necklaces I could give Mélanie Melbourne, necklaces that would glisten in the candlelight against black silk, while we eat our whale carpaccio, in the evening, at the Funken Restaurant (during the day, we'd have gone out, snuggled together, in search of white bears).

"Something along the lines of the Katanga secession, but better" is what they asked me for back at company headquarters in Antwerp. I mention that for those few, probably all senile, for whom the names Moïse Tschombé and Patrice Lumumba still mean something. I'm no spring chicken myself (I scrutinize my face in the rectangular mirror hung above the pale wood desk and all of a sudden I'm struck by an unpleasant budding resemblance to Daladier.[2] Jesus! The floppy spinelessness of age!). Having myself taken part in various struggles for decolonization (though that's another story, which I'll tell later on), I immediately understood what he meant. So I got in touch with Ilyuchinsk, who put together a gang of two hundred skinheads. The problem with Ilyuchinsk is that, even though he's great at this kind of casting, subtlety isn't his strong suit. He didn't learn the art of war from Sun Tzu, in other words. To Lenin's question, "What is to be done?," he's got only one answer: "Send in the tanks." "But Gricha, think about it for a minute," I tell him. "Why not try something more gradual." He looks at me like I

---

2   Daladier: President of the Council of Ministers under the Third Republic, known as "the bull of the Vaucluse," a phony tough guy who lost his nerve in front of Hitler in Munich. I might mention that this reference is comprehensible only for that category of reader, designated above as "rare and probably senile," who also remember Tschombé and Lumumba. *(EN)*

just made a particularly filthy proposition. "What I mean is, you have to have tanks, sure, but only as a last resort. Before getting up there, you need to come up with a pretext." He digs one of his enormous fingers into the wrinkled, reddish hole that stands in for his right ear[3]: a sign that he's thinking. A pretext? *Kakoï prréttiext?* He doesn't get it. What pretext?

> *Text handwritten on a series of four postcards* ("Svalbard, Longyearbyen 78° 10' N. lat.").

---

3 The parenthetical remark, "He has a red hole on the right side," a somewhat misquoted Rimbaud line, has been scratched out. *(EN)*

28

Room 331, Hôtel des Vagues, 9 Boulevard de l'Océan, Arcachon:

On occasion, in order to satisfy Mélanie Melbourne's persistent obsession, I pretend to suddenly remember room 211 of the Hotel Crystal in Nancy, and I describe to her what is in fact a completely different room, sometimes located on the other side of the planet. Invariably, she sees through my ploy. Thus, that evening (after a leisurely day spent bird-watching on the Somme bay, we're back in our rather modest room in the "Villa les Sarcelles," a rooming house in Le Crotoy), that same evening, since she's raising the issue once again, with a doggedness that I sense is bordering now on insanity, I declare that I've, after all, just so happened to have come across, in some old, forgotten notebook, a description of room 211. And, well, it's not much of a room. It's only about 7 x 5 meters, I tell her. Oh my God, it's a real mishmash of blues! The walls and ceiling are done in a baby-blue fabric, the door frames are painted royal blue, the floor is carpeted in navy blue speckled with white motifs suggestive of cuneiform characters. The entrance forms a little hallway where, on the right, before the bathroom door, there are two closets done in a plush fabric with a blue and mauve herringbone pattern.

In the room proper, along the left-hand wall, there is first of all the pale blue laminate casing, with copper green ribbing, on the minibar, atop which, as usual, sits the television, of a not-so-usual brand, Odeon; then there's a flip-down desk made of the same material, with mirrors oddly buttressed on either side above it, and a stool with a blue imitation-leather cushion, with the box of macaroons from the Macaron Sisters on top, I fib shamelessly (in fact, I know very well that I'm actually describing a room in the Hotel des Vagues in Arcachon, where there are no macaroons at all—at best, some *cannelés*). In the corner to the left, an armchair of lacquered blue wood with imitation leather cushions.

The king-size bed abuts the right-hand wall, I continue. On either side, nightstands each have a little white clay lamp vaguely resembling the Pharos of Alexandria, or a very squat obelisk, topped by a very flared, conical, white fabric lampshade (so she wants details, does she? Well, here come your details!). The bedspread, a wide rib fabric, is printed in a pattern that could be described as geometrically leafy, fleur-de-lys-ish, in gray-blue-green . . . And what are you doing in this room? she cuts in without warning. Uh, well . . . I'm talking with Grygor Ilyuchinsk, a kind of Russian Mafioso (in fact, I spent the night with Pashmina Pachelbel in that room in the Hotel des Vagues). An ex-military man. He's looking for a client to sell nuclear heads to, and he found out that I know the cardiologist of the Great Leader of Rpop#%µ©!!¾œ□2&,[1] one of the few people, if not the only person, that he trusts entirely, a real ace, Japanese, actually, with whom . . . well, it's a long story, which I'll tell when

---

1 Scratched out, illegible. To each his interpretation. To that effect, see "room" 34, note 2. *(EN)*

the time comes, perhaps. I call him, and within four hours, he's managed to awaken his patient, I won't say *his illustrious patient,* that would be a bit much, who was sleeping in the arms of his recently appointed Army Chief of Staff (the former having been executed by his orders a few weeks earlier), and, well, I'll spare you the details, but the deal was clinched. But that's . . . immoral, objected Mélanie. I adore Mélanie Melbourne's naïveté. Listen, Zibeline, I tell her (Zibeline is my nickname for her), I needed the money. For you, as usual. You were still being held prisoner, then—I don't even remember now who by. The Colombian FARC guerillas, I think. If you think my royalties are enough to pay off your serial ransom demands . . . This makes her uncomfortable. You didn't say anything about what you could see from the window, that's the part I like best. Talk about the windows, she tells me, to change the subject. The beach, and Cap Ferret straight ahead, I reply, carelessly, and scarcely have the words passed my lips than I realize my enormous, irreparable blunder. If only she would just . . . I try to stray from the issue, there are curt—You said it! A beach in Nancy! Cap Ferret! Anything else? She leaps to her feet, grabs her cheap little pink plastic raincoat, opens the door, blows me an ironic kiss, and she's already down the hallway.

> *Text handwritten on the back of blank identity cards, devoid of data or photographs, probably forgeries.*

29

Room of Doors, Hotel Labyrinth:[1]

The double wooden doors, coated in peeling paint, a color between lead and copper green, and fitted with a sliding iron latch
and a little round brass doorknob, give access to an antechamber, at the back of which a roughly varnished wooden door (a
sloppy job full of dark streaks) opens onto a vestibule measuring
about 3 x 3 meters, lit from the left by a transom in frosted glass
and framed in royal blue. A two-toned wooden door, mahogany
red and oak brown, on which the number 23 is painted in white,
opens on the other side into a corridor along which there are
three more doors: the one on the left, lacquered in cream, is
fitted with a peephole and a guard chain, and the one on the
right, in plywood, is fitted with a handle whose poorly drilled
screw-holes leave it dangling precariously. The third door,
straight ahead, is set into an arch framed by two Doric pilasters, all coated in dark lacquer, almost black. Should you push
through this door, you find yourself in a small entryway, about 2
x 2 meters, lit by a recessed spotlight in the ceiling with the door
to the bathroom on your left, in a coat of grainy cream paint and
set in a brushed aluminum frame. If you open it . . . oh, but that's
not allowed. This door is not to be opened! It's forbidden! Even
so . . . No! But really, what goes on in the bathrooms anyway—
why is this rule so strict? Why doesn't anyone ever just open

---

1   Followed by an illegible address. *(EN)*

the door and walk in? It's very strange. Is there something they want kept hidden? Do they open into . . . into room 211 of the Hotel Crystal, for instance? There's no use insisting or arguing. There are plenty of stories that tell of the untimely demise of those who failed to comply with the rule against opening the forbidden doors. So, if you go back through the door framed by the dark wood pilasters, and then through the door on the right (which is now on the left—I mean, the door with the dangling handle), you enter a small corridor that is closed at the far end by a wooden door with diamond-shaped molding, and gold metallic handle and chain. You then put your ear to the door, and you believe you hear . . . it's very indistinct and far away, but . . . could it be crying, pleading? It calls to mind (and I shiver to think of it) that poem by Larbaud where he imagines that somewhere in a hotel in Mexico City, where he is staying, "in a room glowing with electric lamps," Atahualpa is being garroted to death, as happened four hundred years before in Caxamarca: "Ah, beware of mistaking one door for another!" So, there's nothing left to do but to retrace your steps, heart pounding, and go back down the corridor and open the left-hand door again (which is now straight ahead): the chain has not been latched, fortunately, and so you find yourself face to face with Pashmina Pachelbel dressed like a chambermaid. What a happy encounter! She hardly has the time to act surprised before you're relieving her of the vacuum cleaner that she's pretending to sweep the floor with, an elephant-gray Formica-like floor, and you're feeling under her little black skirt. She's wearing the classic black stockings and garter belt. You shove her against a door fitted with a peephole, a door made of pale Havana brown wood, which, under the combined weight of your entwined bodies, suddenly gives way. And there you are, lying one atop the other, a little bruised but not too much, on a rather comfortable beige carpet sprinkled with grayish-green lines. You take advantage of this circumstance. You get up, put yourselves back in order, not annoyed in the least, and, whistling a happy tune, go through a door, then another, and still another . . . one painted in cream, fitted with a peephole and a chain latch, another in waxed red wood, and another whose two panes of frosted glass allow a milky light to filter through, all suddenly evoking a line from Borges: *"Hay una puerta que he cerrado hasta el fin del mundo,"* "There is a door that I have closed up until the end of the world." Just then, the door on the other side, the one painted pearl gray on battleship gray, begins to pivot slowly . . . you're now in a corridor done in pink moiré. A mirror hangs on the wall, you look into it and discover, unsurprised, the X-ray photograph of your head taken at Forumin Lääkäriasema, on Mannerheimintie in Helsinki, one day in October during the last century.

> *Text handwritten on four postcards* ("The Chapel of the Holy Trinity," "Pors-Even/Paimpol/The Port and the Bay," "Ile de Bréhat/The Cross of Saint Michel," and "Pors-Even/Return of the Fishing Vessels").

30

Room 522, Ma'in Spa Hotel, Madaba, Jordan:

The front door, in a matte finish wood, opens into a hallway of about 3 x 1 meters. On the right is the minibar in a pale wood casing, surmounted by two shelves. Then the closet, three doors in Havana brown wood. Facing you as you enter is the door to the bathroom. In the ceiling, recessed panels, the air-conditioning vent, and a spotlight.

The room itself measures about 6 x 5 meters. The floor is done in large cream-colored tiles, the walls are painted in a grainy eggshell color. A pale ochre band under- and over-scored in faded green runs about 2.5 meters from the floor, about twenty centimeters from the ceiling, which is white. Along this band, one reads, in more or less Gothic script, very pale green, a repeated inscription that I can't manage to decipher: *In Fufnur X alter est:* what in the world is this all about? A secret password?

To the right, past the closet, a luggage rack of the same Havana brown wood, covered in a rough carpet, green with large white dots. Then the desk, long, again in Havana brown wood, on which is set a rather attractive lamp—a hammered metal ball, a white fabric shade—and a Sharp television. A mirror in a wooden frame faces the chair, which is upholstered in a pale orange fabric. As I scrutinize my face in it, I recall that there was once a time when I didn't pay attention to the quality of mirrors, when I hadn't yet noticed that certain mirrors send back a cruel image, while others flatter and embellish (and it's the former that are accurate, since the flattery is only due to the erasure or smoothing over of certain features). Under the desk, a wastepaper basket in cream-colored plastic.

Facing you, on entering, the window takes up an entire wall: two stationary glass panes set in black metal frames, and on either side two matching ones, though these slide open and shut. Two layers of curtains are hung in front of this bay window, the first in gray plastic, the second cut in a vertically striped fabric in beige, yellow, and ochre. Outside, on the balcony rimmed with a black wrought-iron guardrail, a white three-legged table and two chairs in white plastic—standard bistro furniture. Beyond, the mountain studded with streetlamps, black against the deep blue sky where a nearly full moon glows. The hotel is located at the bottom of a gorge, right on the Dead Sea, at an "altitude" of 200 meters below sea level. Streetlights line the road that winds down to the water. To the left, a rock face, steep and smooth, very close, is sculpted by spring water cascading from high above.

On the left-hand side, facing the window, a large double bed, covered by a blanket in beige squares with some pattern I'm declining to describe, blue, butter, or brown on an orange background. The headboard is a thick plank of Havana brown wood, plain and unadorned. There are two nightstands of the same plain wood, equipped with a single drawer, each holding a lamp like the one on the desk. The left-hand one also has a black, touchtone telephone of some unknown brand. The ring is extremely discreet, something like gurgling bubbles; we're in a spa hotel, after all. Still, it does manage to stir me out of despondency. It's Schmelk. A few seconds later, he's knocking softly at my door in the company of Barabas and Pomdapi,[1] the twin sons of the dictator of a neighboring country, and Pashmina Pachelbel. They're a sight to behold: Schmelk, in a slate-gray suit, looking as always as if he's swallowed his umbrella, carrying his invention under his arm in a hatbox; Pashmina wearing purple fishnet stockings with stiletto heels and a very low-cut fuchsia dress; the twins in their white spa bathrobes and slippers, each with a whiskey bottle sticking out of a pocket. They have heavy moustaches, thickset chins, and look a little like General Alcazar in *Tintin*. Pashmina was the one who, under circumstances that I will leave to your imagination, came to know them, and put us in touch. The ingenious Czech engineer has invented a spy drone no bigger than a fly, and what's more, equipped with an infrared, high-resolution camera—a jewel of miniaturized technology that the neighboring dictator is extremely interested in acquiring. While Schmelk is unpacking his material, plugging black boxes and cables behind the TV set, the twins settle onto the bed, Pashmina between them. One hand on their bottles, the other where you might imagine. Try as I might not to be insanely jealous (and you're better off not bothering where Pashmina's concerned), these two are starting to annoy me. They're also getting a little hot under their collars. Schmelk delivers his spiel as if everything were normal: Argus—that's the name of the drone—has a two-hour range of flight time, and is so small that

1   See Michaux. *(AN)*

it's absolutely undetectable . . . the only problem is that you have to be careful not to misplace it, you just have to be a little organized, etc. Barabas takes a slug of whiskey and burps; Pomdapi is attempting to grab one of Pashmina's breasts, which limply resists, as it were. Throwing the windows wide open (you can hear the rush of spring water cascading off the cliff), Schmelk has his robot take off from the back of his hand. Bzzzz . . . While Argus is circling upwards, greenish but very sharp images stream across the television screen: you can make out mountains, the luminous snaking road, the hotel nestled in its basin, and then, like a sheet of tin in moonlight, the Dead Sea. At this, even the twins sit up and take notice. On the other side, Israel. Can it drop bombs, too? asks Barabas. No, the size of the thing doesn't allow for that. Oh. Too bad (he burps). Now, Schmelk has his drone return. Pomdapi wants to handle the landing. Well, it's just that . . . It takes a little practice. Mr. Moustache is pissed off, he's already flown planes before, driven Ferraris, tanks, he wants to do the landing. He's completely plastered. He pulls a gun out from under his bathrobe and starts waving it around. Resigned, Schmelk gives him a quick rundown of how to work the remote, then, extending a collapsible rod, he attaches to it the butterfly net that makes it possible . . . *that's supposed to make it possible* to catch Argus. On the screen, the façade of the hotel looms larger, then, in jumpy flashes, the window of room 522. "To the left, to the left," orders Schmelk. Too late! Images of what looks like a snowy cave jump and blink for a second or two, then the screen goes blank as Pomdapi drops to the floor, screaming. The moron got the drone stuck in his ear. On the bed, Barabas is doubled over, laughing.

> *Text handwritten on three sheets of stationary, "Embassy of France / Department of Culture and Scientific Cooperation / 802 RELC Building / 30 Orange Grove Road / Singapore 258352."*

31

Room 17, Peacock Inn, 20 Bayard Lane, Princeton, New Jersey:

Arlette Harlowe hasn't always been a wealthy heiress. I'm talking about before she met Mr. Colgate, and particularly before (which should be obvious) she had him killed (in fact, she arranged to have him eaten by an alligator, a dreadful mishap!). She was a voluptuous, eyelash-batting, platinum-blonde college student. She made a point of strolling around campus in a tight T-shirt and cutoff jeans. With ankles that looked like they were crafted by a luthier (planted in a pair of Nikes, unfortunately), shapely thighs and calves, sleek and shiny as fish (it may look like I'm repeating myself, going on about this, but bear with me! It starts out the same, but later on it's very different, you'll see.) I was giving lectures at the university, and she came up to me after one of them to ask for some clarifications, something about metonymy in Proust, with Gerard Genette, you get the picture, and one thing led to another . . . I'll always remember, down to the tiniest detail, "as if I were there," the little room we shared for a whole month: I came away not only with some poignant memories, but also—and I can say this with assurance—the working capital for a sizable chunk of my life.

The front door, behind which your feet were greeted by a semicircular doormat in the shape of a peacock spreading its tail feathers, opened onto a little vestibule wallpapered in a pattern of red peonies and green foliage, with a ceiling sloping to the left. Brown carpet. Opposite the bathroom door, which opened on the left, there was a white rattan chair with a pale blue cushion. A door equipped with an Atlas brand "Doorman" gave access to the room itself, rather on the small side (about 4.5 x 4.5 meters), with sloping ceilings on either side. The carpet was green, the wallpaper, quite attractive (as was that in the entryway, in fact), printed in delicate little mauve and blue flowers at the end of long, twisting stems. A ceiling fan/light unit was the only truly ugly thing in the room. Against the left-hand wall as you entered was an antique cast-iron radiator encased in a metal cage. Out the small double-hung window, in front of which a set of Venetian blinds slide (with some difficulty), doubled by embroidered sheer curtains, you could see the windows of the floor opposite, fitted with rather strange, fluorescent pink shutters, and some fake slate roofing shingles, other windows, other houses, trees, and Bayard Lane to the right. In front of the window (making access particularly arduous) was a wooden chest of drawers, painted white.

On the outcropping of wall facing the door hung a naïve little painting of a horse-drawn sleigh against a snowy landscape; two figures collect maple syrup in buckets attached to tree trunks. Recesses on either side were particularly inviting: on the left, beneath the sloping roof, on the glass top of a four-drawer white rattan desk, was a Zenith television, and a lamp with a pale green amphora-shaped base and a white skirted shade; in front of the desk was a white rattan chair with a pale green flecked cushion. To the right, a round night table, rattan, with a baffling radio-alarm clock that (like all devices of that type) I have no idea how to use, and a lamp whose long, black fluted stem bears a brass peacock (its long tail forming a scored "S" like a dollar sign, $, with the stem of the lamp) and a little white skirted shade.

Against the third wall were the twin beds, each covered in a white bedspread (and fortunately pushed together to form one large bed). To the right, a little wooden table painted white, with one drawer and four slim legs, holding a black Panasonic telephone. The last wall (where the front door was located) had an oval mirror, with no frame. Sometimes, during our trysts, it would reflect a raised leg, an arched torso, a rounded back.

One day, in post-coital repose, Arlette reached into her Indian bag all studded with little stitched-on mirrors, and pulled out some pictures from her vacation in Old Europe. In one of them—it was from Rome, in front of the Trevi Fountain (*ô lieu commun*, I thought, *in petto*)—she was posing cheek-to-cheek with some Latin lover type dressed in a skintight black T-shirt, soon to be *the* hipster attire. Who's that guy? I asked, not without a hint of irritation. I expected him to be a photographer, a cinematographer, or at very least, a writer, but she answered, amid peals of laughter (we'd had quite a bit to drink and smoke), that he was a priest. His name was Luigi Fottorino, and he'd taken her to see the Sistine Chapel (she called it "the Sweet Sextine"), they'd had grappas on the Campo dei Fiori, and with her, he'd discovered the wonders of love[1] in a hotel in the Trastevere district. Well now, isn't that interesting!

I filed that tidbit away for future use. Ten years later, when I read in the *Osservatore romano* that the smart, young Monsignor Luigi Fottorino had been appointed to a key Vatican position in the Secretary of State's office, my plan was as good as hatched. I got on a plane for Rome where, thanks to a cunning ruse, I was granted an audience with the Monsignore, who had no trouble understanding that, starting from now, he'd do well to avoid getting on my bad side. He was very smart, in fact: a clever boy, as Arlette said. Very astute. And thus began the despicable life of a man who, had he not been poisoned (by whom? I have some serious suspicions, but this is neither the time nor place—later, perhaps), would undoubtedly have ended up as Pope. I won't give any details, but suffice it to say that the world is full of powerful people ready to pay whatever it takes to get the inside story on Vatican politics, and I had this Fottorino on a leash. Like they say about dogs, "he did it where I told him to." Poor Luigi. He served me well. *Requiescat in pace!*

> *Text handwritten on two pages ripped from* Under the Volcano *by Malcolm Lowry, Penguin Books.*

---

1 As the accepted expression goes (nothing to do with the sacraments). *(AN)*

32

Room 229, Novotel Orisha, Boulevard de la Marina, Cotonou:

The front door, in light wood, is equipped with a Blount[1] and a gold chain lock. On the left-hand side of a rather spacious corridor (about 2 x 3 meters) are two doors: the first, lacquered white with a light gray border, opens into the toilet; and the second, the bathroom door, in every way identical to the first, is separated from it by a wall panel where, below a circular sconce in white frosted glass, there hangs a tall, narrow mirror. The colors (orange and grayish-green) and patterns (wormy, bacillus-like) of the carpet look a great deal like vomit, as is often the case in hotel rooms. The walls are painted in a grainy white. The ceiling is about 2.5 meters high.

The right-hand wall as you enter runs all the way to the windowed wall, about 9 meters away, which is to say that this room is roomy. Facing the toilet and bathroom doors, they've set up a wardrobe of sorts that consists of two dihedrals face to face, a simple design, elegant lines. Next comes a low chest made of

---

1 I don't know the actual name of this device, consisting of a piston mounted on an articulated stem, used to automatically close a door. I only recall that one of the first bits of writing that impressed me as a child—along with *E pericoloso sporgersi* on train windows—was printed on this device: "You needn't shut the door, that's what the Blunt is for." The command perhaps drew some of its potency from the formulation in a (near) perfect Alexandrine (or two perfect hexameters). Whatever the case, the name Blunt (or Blount?) has remained linked to this device, which is perhaps called an "automatic door closer." I have no idea, really (in the United States, I'm pretty sure they call it by the brand name "Doorman"). *(AN)*

melamine plastic panels with wooden guards on the angles. The piece serves as a luggage rack, with three slats of wood secured to the wall as protective bumpers. I set my garment bag down on it, with its ghoulish contents. After that comes the minibar, encased in the same plastic paneling, then the long desktop counter whose far end is supported by a chest with two large drawers, upon which sit an Alcatel touchtone telephone, a lamp composed of a heavy, white cylindrical metallic base, topped by a half-sphere in white opalescent plastic, and finally a Blue Sky TV set. Two chairs in pale wood with ochre plastic seats are set facing this work space, over which is hung a reproduction in a glass and pale wood frame of Matisse's *Young Girl in a White Dress*, dated June '41.

In the middle of the wall facing the door is a pair of sliding glass doors set in a brushed aluminum frame, about 2 x 2 meters. They open onto a little balcony measuring about 2 x 1 meters, with a railing painted oxblood red. From left to right, one can see the following: a building under construction, bristling with rebar, two cranes hovering overhead; the nearest warehouses on the port; a stand of young coconut trees, right under the balcony; further off, the beach swarming with people, edged with breakers that seem to stir up a light mist, and still further beyond, the turquoise sea, where five cargo ships are at anchor; on the far right, still more beach, breakers, the sea, and beneath some palm trees a glimpse of the swimming pool. Sheer curtains and mauve cloth drapes run all along the sliding doors.

The wall perpendicular to the window is shielded, up to a height of 1.5 meters, by two panels of white melamine plastic framed in pale wood. Up against the one closest to the window, there's a sofa protected by a slipcover in a mauve and green diamond pattern, with three large orange cushions forming the back. The second panel serves as the headboard, the bed measuring about 1.75 x 2 meters, rather low-slung, covered in the same mauve and green fabric. Little nightstands on either side, each surmounted by a white opalescent half-globe sconce. A third melamine panel is set vertically, for no obvious reason, in the corner with the bathroom wall, which is bare except for the thermostat.

This morning I went to the Dantokpa market, along the lagoon. I wandered through the displays of dead, mummified animals, sold for voodoo ceremonies. Birds, chameleons, frogs, toads, snakes, heads of dogs, deer, monkeys, civets. Hideous grins, empty eye sockets, teeth clenched over shreds of lip, cutting through the flesh, glistening against the blackish, leathery meat. Heads, snouts and muzzles. A whole, gruesome witch's Sabbath. Bodies shrunken, boiled, parched, all in the sour stench, the stink of old mops that cadavers give off. I thought of the *Ballade des pendus*. I purchased a large monkey, wrinkled as dried fruit, pretty foul. The face seemed oddly familiar, something nice about it, almost friendly, however unsightly. Suddenly . . . it wasn't possible . . . and yet, there it was. I had just sat down at the canal's edge, took a generous swig from my whiskey flask—a gift from Mélanie Melbourne, which I always keep in my front, right-hand shirt pocket (where it saved my life once in Kabul, repelling some shrapnel that would otherwise have sliced into my heart like a can opener—but that's another story, which

I'll tell another time, perhaps)—and I started to unwrap the mummy, which the vendor had bound up in newsprint. And, God almighty! There could be no doubt. What I was holding there—this fetid, smoked piece of meat—bore a strong, almost outlandish resemblance to Papadiamantides.

Poor Themistocles. His last smuggling job had done him in. He had chartered a little Ukrainian tanker, the *African Queen,* onto which he was going to load some illegal oil in Nigeria. He was in cahoots with a gang with ties to an ethnic faction of the army, which was siphoning off Chevron's and Texaco's pipelines, among others, in the marshland of the Niger Delta, by filling up barges that would then transfer the cargo to his rusty old tub. After which Themistocles got rid of the stuff at the port of Cotonou. It was a risky business, because the oil companies obviously had no intention of letting themselves be fleeced without doing something about it—and because ripping off Big Oil in a country where even a two-bit shoplifter often ends up getting burned alive between two tires, well, while you can win big sometimes, it can also be deadly. Never mind that Themistocles's associates were no angels themselves, and that divvying up the profits, on every trip, led to arguments where there was little room for philosophy. Which is why it surprised no one (least of all me, who was in on the deal) when we learned, three months ago, that an explosion had wrecked the *African Queen* while it was unloading in Cotonou. The boat burned for two days, all crew members present either perished or were declared missing. Among the missing was Themistocles. Themistocles whose . . . whose charred remains I was holding in my lap?

Now, let's just think a moment. I open the minibar and pour myself a gin and tonic. I, for one, think better with a drink, which is not an excuse just anyone can give. I put the thing in the garment bag on the white melamine chest. Let's not lose our cool here. It could very well be, after all, that the official version is true: a Ukrainian threw a cigarette butt into an empty tank, and ka-boom! It's the most plausible explanation, in fact. Except . . . it could just as well be a case of Big Oil getting even. Or maybe it was our own "associates"? And what if . . . here's an idea . . . what if Antonomarenko was in on it? What if he had peddled his services to . . . to this group or that? To this group AND that? After all, he's Ukrainian too. Could he have let something slip, drinking with his comrades in some bar in Port Harcourt? But first of all, is it Themistocles who's in my garment bag or not? Because if it's really him, it wouldn't be out of the question that . . . that I didn't just stumble across this . . . thing, this morning in Dantokpa: maybe *they* actually stuck me with it? An inexpensive warning. Right, it's coming back to me now . . . it was the vendor, actually, who called me over. Nothing suspicious there in and of itself, mind you. A white guy strolling around Dantokpa, and someone gives him a sales pitch. So, it's time to decide: is it him or not? I open the zipper. How did I let myself get talked into buying this fiendish thing that I'm trying so hard not to recognize as Themistocles Papadiamantides? Only, here's the problem: have you ever seen a monkey with steel teeth?

Text handwritten on four sheets of "Novotel Orisha" stationary.

33

Royal Suite, Hotel Crystal, 5 Rue Chanzy, Nancy:

Shortly before,[1] sensing that the moment of truth was drawing nigh, I decided to gather all my friends together, for the last time perhaps, in my suite at the Hotel Crystal. On the appointed day, at the appointed hour, I greeted my friends, arm in arm with Zibeline, ravishing in a little black dress that set off her fine porcelain complexion and sorrowful eyes. Ilyuchinsk arrived first, in punctual military fashion, at 19:30 sharp. He was wearing his customary military fatigues, but he'd stuck a daisy in his ear— "to honor the young lady," he said, sneering in the direction of Mélanie, with the intention, one assumes, of smiling. Papadiamantides followed soon after, disguised as Captain Haddock: turtleneck sweater, cap, ouzo bottle in his pocket. Next came Pashmina, somewhat overdressed in a tight, fake zebra skirt and leopard bustier, whose hardly allegorical message seemed to be "hunting season is now open." Crook, holding the already pretty well-lubricated Iskandar Arak-Bar by the arm, guided the latter into the room. Arlette Harlowe, who had long ago forgiven me the Incarnación affair, had had her first face lift: time marches on, Madame. The last to show was Pavel Schmelk. Even for this little get-together, the ingenious engineer still clung to his "East-

---

1   Before what? We don't know, nor will we ever. The most we can state with any certainty is that, at the time of this scene, 1) Papadiamantides is still alive, 2) The Chukotka debacle had taken place shortly before, and 3) Arlette Harlowe is no longer in the first bloom of youth. *(EN)*

ern Bloc" look, wearing a brown double-breasted suit under a gabardine raincoat, a felt hat—too small—perched on his shiny bald head.

The party was a very merry affair. After downing a great many shots of straight vodka and smashing a number of champagne flutes over his shoulder, Gricha told us the story as to why his expedition in Chukotka had failed: the riots that had followed the soccer match between Spartak Anadyr and Glasgow Rangers, won by the Scottish team 12–0, had provided the grounds for his operation. So far, so good. Unfortunately, "as a shortcut," he had brought his tanks across the frozen river, when craaak! the ice gave way. The story had him doubled over laughing, even though nearly all his skinheads had drowned. In his opinion, they should have been able to pass: didn't they run train tracks over Lake Baikal during the Russian-Japanese War? Crook, also in high spirits, tried to interest us in his latest deal: a scrap metal company based in Malta, serving as a front for a virtual holding company registered in the Bahamas, and whose capital, composed half of stock options, half of consolidated Russian loans (here Ilyuchinsk pricked up his sole ear), would be shared equally between an import-export company based in the Caiman Islands (this time, Arlette Harlowe was the one who could not suppress a smile) and an Anglo-Chinese agribusiness joint venture headquartered on Jersey (seaweed, nuoc mam, rice alcohol, etc.), laundering the savings collected over the Internet of the wives of a few African dictators, all of which was supposed to act as a shelter for Overseas Catering, of which Crook was the CEO and sole board member, which was the sole supplier (thanks to his friend Prince Ibn ******, whom he used to play cricket with back at Oxford) of liquor and call girls to the Saudi royal family. "Clever, don't you think?" he asked Schmelk, who had understood not a word. Pashmina, who likewise comprehended nothing, showed some interest in Overseas Catering's mission statement, saying (while taking a drag on her cigarette holder, not so much to enjoy the smoke as to suck in her cheeks and round out her lips, which were still large and lovely) that she could "pull some strings." There was a tense moment, though quickly defused, when Iskandar, whose mood was increasingly dark, attempted to swipe Themistocles's ouzo bottle, which was sticking out of his pocket. Themistocles didn't take it lightly, and they were soon at each other's throats, feathers flying, but were pulled apart, and were drinking to one another's health a few minutes later. Arlette Harlowe was starting to experience some doubt as to her sex appeal, and moreover she found it terrifically exciting to meet a former colonel of the Red Army, the somewhat spectacular Grisha, with his ear like a whale's blowhole. She kept asking him to pull up her dress zipper in back, and everyone could see how this was all going to turn out. As expected, it wasn't long before they slipped away. Schmelk, who didn't drink, concealed beneath his fixed smile a slight look of disgust. Zibeline assumed a martyr's air, but a martyr pleased with her fate, unlikely to reprimand. Iskandar tried to recite some Mallarmé in Arabic. There were holes.

All that, of course, is pure fabrication. This little gathering never took place. I've told you a dozen times that I don't have ANY memory of the Hotel Crystal. The Hotel Crystal is a vacant space, a warehouse of imaginary merchandise, a Novel Hotel, as it were. A suite in the Hotel Crystal . . . and you fell for it! And yet, it's not the kind of hotel that has suites . . . Oh, I know what you're going to say now: that I DO remember SOME-THING after all? No, not unless you call "something" the fact that it's a modest establishment.[2] That much I do remember. And also the box of Macaron Sisters macaroons. And actually . . . I'm not even so sure about that. Where does that name come from, to begin with, "the Macaron Sisters?" I seem to recall it was printed on the box, but the dictionary here says that maca-ron comes from the Venetian macarone, macaroni, so this thing about the sisters is starting to sound rather unlikely. Maybe it was a box of bergamot oranges instead? In Nancy, isn't that maybe a little more plausible?

> *Text handwritten on the pages torn out of* Das Neue Testament / Le Nouveau Testament / The New Testament, *Internationaler Gideonbund / L'Association Internationale des Gédéons / The Gideons International.*

---

2   Which is not all that much, we should point out. *(EN)*

34

Room 11XX, City Hotel, Bolivar 160, Buenos Aires:

The room measures about 5 x 5 meters, the walls are hung in a plastic imitation fabric, alternating strips of moiré, horizontal slashes, fine vertical stripes, etc., in a pinkish rose color reminiscent of cartilage. The floor is done in blue carpet. The door opens directly into the room, and two panes of frosted glass let in light from the outside hallway, which is both pleasant and unpleasant. To the right of the door, in the middle of the wall, the closet juts out, from floor to ceiling, at a width of about 1.7 meters. The wall to the left has the door to the bathroom, the same model as the front door—with the two frosted glass panes—though a little shorter.

Two large windows, shielded by some stuck Venetian blinds and a chiffon curtain, also jammed, are located on the wall opposite the front door: each is divided into two pivoting panes, or panes which used to pivot, each the same size. Way down below (we're on the eleventh floor), you can see terraced roofs encumbered with cisterns, ventilation shafts and ductwork, dish antennae, etc. A few potted plants, laundry hung out to dry. Buildings seemingly thrown together any old way, unevenly calibrated, bristling with tall antennae around which radiate clusters of cable, the dome and twin steeples of a church, and then, off in the distance, the red-and-white striped smokestacks of some large factory (probably a power station), and the muddy waters of the

Rio de la Plata. The dominant feature of the surrounding area is the phenomenal noise from Bolivar and the adjacent streets, Perú, Yrigoyen, Diagonal Sur, etc.: the rumble of the colectivos, car horns, the background hum of traffic, police sirens, etc. Nearby clock towers strike every quarter hour.

Furnishings consist of a huge mahogany-colored bed, fortunately unencumbered by fancy trimmings, and covered, thankfully, by a white bedspread. On either side, two little single-drawer night tables, each bearing a wooden lamp with a white, cylindrical shade. A color photograph hangs above the bed, in a wooden frame, showing a snowy alpine landscape: a winding path, a house, glistening trees.

Opposite the bed, on either side of the bathroom door: first, on the left, a luggage rack made out of wood and straps, and a mirror framed in wood. I gaze into it. My hair is thin enough for light to pass through it. An old plucked rooster. If Aurelia were still alive, would she recognize me? So many years have passed since we first met, at the El Ideal bar where she was a waitress . . . So many years, as well, since my conversations with Borges . . . I had never come back to Buenos Aires. Then, on the right, a no-frills table, mahogany-colored, with three drawers, each equipped with brass knobs, on which sits a little TV set. Above hangs another alpine landscape: a lake with snowy banks. An armchair upholstered in a gray-and-pink striped fabric, and a ceiling light in starry, frosted glass completes the décor.

This is the room where Antonomarenko committed suicide. We'll probably never know why for sure. We have our pick of reasons, as he had his. He might have been just as tortured by regrets over his failed undertakings as by remorse for his successful ones. Though he never managed to knock me off, he did eliminate (or that's my theory, anyway) a *papabile*. And though he didn't succeed in preventing Papadiamantides and me from smuggling out blueprints of the Proton rocket in a can of caviar, he did, in the end, manage to bag poor old Themistocles. He tried in vain to take his cut on the ransom paid for Mélanie Melbourne to Ansar al Islam, though it seems he did get his commission on the sale of nuclear warheads to the Rpop#%µ©!!¾œ□2&.[1] He was the one, in fact, who made me cross out . . . [2] I'm not the one who bumped him off, don't go putting words in my mouth. In fact, for a long time, I believed (and spread the word around)

---

1 Crossed out, illegible. Your guess is as good as ours. *(EN)*

2 Crossed out, illegible. We have long wondered about the motives for this recurring self-censorship, which is made all the stranger for being completely ineffectual, since it would seem that just about anyone could guess that North Korea was the consignee, and the instigator, of the nuclear arms smuggling operation. But let us not forget the other learned commentators on the scene, who have proposed alternative interpretations, such as Gustavo Robinet (reference to Ignacio Ramonet, editor-in-chief of the monthly *Le Monde Diplomatique* —Translator's note), in *Le Monde de la diplomatie,* who thinks the Principality of Monaco can be discerned beneath the inky cross-hatching, and recognizes Prince Rainier in the figure of the Great Leader, alias the Beloved Father. The real question, in our opinion, goes as follows: does this (fake) dissimulation result from threats issued by Pyongyang *via* Antonomarenko (a thesis that the author puts forward here), or on the contrary, should we be seeing in these erasures the result of some successful blackmailing on the author's part of the North Korean authorities (or Monegasque, if we follow Gustavo Robinet's interpretation): "I'll cross out your name, but it's going to cost you however many million dollars"? By now, the reader has probably gleaned that the latter hypothesis (confirmed, by the way, by Mme. ***) is the one we prefer—particularly since the author prompts us a tad too forcefully to adopt the other. *(EN)*

that he had hung himself, when in fact he jumped out a window. Did I say that the windows didn't open anymore? No, that's not what I said. I was talking about "pivoting panes, or panes which used to pivot." Don't go putting words in my mouth. I don't even feel particularly gratified at the realization that Antonomarenko won't be thwarting my plans anymore. Sure, I'm relieved. But I'm also experiencing something like loss. He'll never cross my path again, that's for sure: but might it not also be true that I've reached the end of that path myself?

Despite the noise, this room, with its height, its light, and especially its unfussy décor, is oddly pleasant.[3]

> *Text handwritten on a mass transit map of Buenos Aires.* ("Guia Peuser, combinaciones de subterraneos y colectivos.")

---

3   This section is remarkable for its inaccuracy. Even the room number remains uncertain: it was we who replaced the entry "Room ???" with "Room 11XX," given the fact, as stated in the second paragraph, that the room is located on the eleventh floor. The author does not follow rigorous descriptive procedure that he otherwise so strictly adheres to, not moving on to a subsequent wall until he has exhausted the previous one, and so forth. Here, everything is tossed in a bit haphazardly, as if by an observer in a hurry (where, for example, is the "armchair upholstered in a gray-and-pink striped fabric" located?) As for the hesitations that characterize the account, which at times amount to contradictions, they are too flagrant to require any further emphasis. These observations have led some to suspect that this text is apocryphal: we, for our part, would not take matters that far. *(EN)*

35

Room 213, The Agnes Hotel, 2-20-1 Kagurazaka, Sinjuku-ku, Tokyo 162-0825:

The front door, painted in dark blue, equipped with a peephole and a chain lock, opens into a hallway of about 3 meters long by 1 meter wide with a black-and-white tiled floor. The walls, like those of the room, are done in a finely crinkled beige skin, imitating leather. The ceiling is washed in a fine beige roughcast plaster: the hallway ceiling has a spotlight and a sprinkler, while the room's has four spotlights and two sprinklers. To the right, midway down the corridor, is the door opening into the bathroom, lacquered in off-white. Further on, a towel-warmer in gold metallic tubing, for which numerous safety instructions are provided in English (*Please do not place dry-cleaned clothes on this device. The oil used to dry-clean may cause fire! Please refrain from using the device when children are in the room!*). If drying towels is so dangerous, perhaps it would be better to do away with them altogether. On the left, there are, in order of appearance, an AEG-brand washing machine built into the wall under a shelf, then a kitchenette with cupboards containing dishes, cooking utensils, etc. All the woodwork is light in color.

The room itself measures about 5 x 5 meters. The floor is carpeted in a crisscrossed pattern of beige and black ribbing that makes it look like a rope rug. The wall extending from the kitchen includes, under a shelf holding a Sanyo microwave oven, a built-in refrigerator, also a Sanyo (Tutu model); next, a three-door closet surmounted by three small cupboards; next, a countertop, where I'm presently writing, facing a mirror in a wood frame reflecting my image: slightly tan, short hair, freshly shaven (closely?), beige linen shirt—almost presentable. A lamp, whose round, gold metallic base, with a stem in the form of a question mark and a white glass shade, sits on the left-hand side of this counter, with a paper napkin dispenser, an ashtray, and a glass on the right.

In the corner of the wall facing the door is a little double-shelved cabinet with a DVD player on the lower shelf and a Toshiba television set on the upper. This wall is taken up almost entirely by a window of about 3 x 1.7 meters, two panes framed in metal, the left-hand one a sliding panel with a screen mounted in front. Beyond a little balcony, you can see, through a persistent drizzle: a wing of the hotel to the left, four pale ochre floors with balconies identical to mine; then straight ahead, a little brick house on a narrow street whose blacktop glistens in the rain, planted with bushes that are perhaps lilacs, leaves glistening as well—a few pink hydrangeas are in bloom around the house. In the middle distance, a tangle of cables striping the gray sky is knotted around a tilted wooden telephone pole. Further off: various buildings, some scaffolding, antennae, the grillwork cage (looking like a gigantic chicken coop) of a driving range. Sheer white curtains and drapes in a heavy beige fabric are mounted on runners over the window, near which is arranged a little round folding table in pale wood.

In the corner of the third wall is a reading chair upholstered in a wide-ribbed beige fabric. Above, a National-brand air-conditioner. Next, a little two-drawer rosewood chest—the top drawer containing, apart from the phone book, *The Teachings of Buddha* and a New Testament, as well as a flashlight, in case of earthquake. On the top, a glass-stemmed lamp on a square, gold metal base, with a white skirted shade atop a golden crest, and a Casio telephone too. Then, in the corner with the last wall, the bed, high and spacious, with a rosewood headboard, covered by a tan bedspread.

The reading I gave two days ago at the French Institute, a stone's throw from here, was followed by the jostling of the young girls in navy blue uniforms and white socks, or in little Prada dresses, or bell-bottom jeans, wearing tennis shoes, clogs, flats, or high heels, with jet black, brown, or bleached hair, straight, braided, or in ribbons, who are usually in attendance at all my public appearances on the archipelago. I've stopped paying much attention to this babbling bunch. I sign books, programs, subway tickets, bikini underwear, I dispense and receive kisses, perfunctorily. But the day before yesterday, something happened. In the first row, ravishing in a black dress that set off her porcelain skin, there was . . . A charming little pinched nose (that you wished you could pinch), an impish mouth, eyes like notched arrows beneath arched brows, hair like microgroove silk tucked behind little ears begging to be bitten: Mitsuko! I'd dreamt of her the previous night, after seeing her on TV in a series entitled *House of Sand:* she played a young woman who called for phone sex when she got bored at home. Ah, how I longed to dispel her ennui! And there she was now, in the first row, her ivory legs crossed, one of them beating in time . . . That delectable pussy . . . A mad desire to thrust my hand into it, my snout . . . But I had to continue my reading, my mind elsewhere, so to speak. I've always loved Japanese girls. Something mysterious about them, a hint of the forbidden. You need only approach one and you immediately imagine her (I do, at least) withdrawing on tiny, sliding feet, eyes lowered, cheeks pink, into a paper labyrinth, whence suddenly emerges some hulking, ironclad figure, giving out guttural shouts and brandishing a sword he's just used to decapitate a few insects in mid-flight. Very exciting. And then, there's that strange pallor to their skin, so fine-grained, so soft, kaolin, un-tanned leather . . . It's as if (I'm going into detail for all those who have never, even inadvertently, touched a Japanese girl), it's as if their bodies were covered entirely in breast-skin.[1]

But Mitsuko's skin is an infinitely more refined substance than even that. A virtually immaterial fabric, woven of sunbeams. The average Japanese girl's skin is sackcloth next to hers. Mitsuko's skin glows ever so slightly in the dark, it shimmers like light on water. It's ionized, iridescent silk, an aurora borealis. I can assert that some moron ending up in bed with her but un-

---

1   Here, it would appear that the author is inspired by certain classics of erotic literature with an Eastern flavor (Pierre Loti?). We must remind the reader that the texts assembled in this collection are nothing but uncorrected drafts, having undergone no revision whatsoever with an eye towards their eventual publication. *(EN)*

able to think of anything better to do could read by the light of her body. Obviously this luminescence is somewhat disturbing, but it's such a delightful disturbance, since this astonishing skin is also as fresh as spring water—to stroke it is to dip one's hands in a fountain. I perform my ablutions, I drink from its source, I swim in its stream, I dive and thrash and gush and foam in her falls. How can she ever put up with, let alone love, or so it seems, my rough hide, my boar-bristles?

I'm writing these lines while Mitsuko is in the bathroom. I wonder whether these will be the last I'll ever write, in fact, since Mitsuko is the mistress of a Yakuza boss, and he's not going to find this little escapade to his liking, should he ever find out about it. As I write, I'm keeping an eye on that alley among the lilacs glistening in the fine drizzle outside. I tap my pocket to feel the reassuring presence of my Glock 17 laser-sight semi-automatic (it shoots smart bullets). There's nothing to distinguish the last wall (behind which is the bathroom) except an unusual device for a hotel room: a white telephone equipped with an LCD screen and options reading Emergency, Stop the Alarm, and Open the Entrance Door. Open the entrance door? Well, I'm not about to do that . . .

Text handwritten on four sheets of stationary, "The Agnes / Hotel and Apartments / Tokyo."

36

Room of windows, Belleviews Hotel:[1]

The room, apparently inspired by an imaginary arrangement found in a book by some screwball writer or other (or so I've been assured),[2] appears as a rotunda about 6 meters high. Circular gangways located at various heights make it possible to benefit from the numerous views afforded by its dozens of windows. Each window is unique, providing a view unlike any other—none of which, incidentally, is anything special. What's remarkable, however, is the sheer number of views, a mystifying attribute that no one as yet has been able to explain. From one of these, you can see some terraced rooftops cluttered with drying laundry far below, among the cisterns and air vents, then some buildings bristling with antennae, from which clusters of cables radiate like shrouds, the dome and twin steeples of a church, and tall red-and-white striped smokestacks on the banks of a muddy river. Out another window, a little paved courtyard where, beneath a lime tree that the wind has practically stripped of its leaves, tables and chairs are stacked, remnants of high

---

1   An address follows, crossed out, then scratched out, now illegible. *(EN)*
2   Despite in-depth research, particularly in the archives of the *Review of Excessive Literature,* as well as in those of SELL (the *Society for the Encouragement of Lunatic Literature*), we have not been able to determine which book (or which author) is referred to here. Undoubtedly it is a work whose very eccentricity has relegated it to obscurity. We would like to thank Professor Lafaurie (*For a Semiotics of the Strange,* Seuil, 1978; *Anthology of Screwball Literature,* Pauvert, 1970) for his help and suggestions. *(EN)*

summer, as well as outdoor bistro terrace heaters. Sometimes, even neighboring windows afford slightly different landscapes, but the resemblances between these induce the viewer to believe they are one and the same. Should you open the blue moiré drapes and sheer curtains, you can get a look at the beach and a section of sea, a little seaside town. One window further down, the coastline has disappeared, cargo ships are at anchor, fishing boats trawl offshore the trash-strewn beach, and on the right, you can see the port. One more window over, behind mauve canvas curtains, is the beach, with turquoise breakers coming in succession, and a swarm of strollers; the port warehouses are now on your left, along with a building under construction, bristling with rebar, two cranes hovering overhead; a shiny-leafed tree—perhaps a rubber tree—which was below the previous window is now replaced by a stand of young coconut trees; and further on, we're still at the shoreline, but it's nighttime now: two lamps have been lit, the faint clinking of halyards against metallic masts comes from the little boats dancing on the black water. Casements open onto a dusty balcony: on the opposite side of the street, at the end of which the sea and a fortress are visible, you can see a colorful though somewhat dilapidated building, in a more or less neo-Florentine style: dry laundry in one window, a carpet in the other. If you look out the adjacent window, everything seems normal at first: there's still a building opposite, though it's a different one. Oddly enough—we've become so accustomed to this inconsistent world—it's this normalcy itself that's surprising. Once you take a closer look, the differences become immediately apparent: street lights are suspended over the pavement by a catenary system, and in place of the sea at the end of the street, you can now see the dark foliage of a park. Slightly below, an open window reveals someone sitting in a black leather swivel chair at a cluttered desk (bottles of mineral water and orange juice, rolls of paper, a computer): a man with medium-length blond hair whose black, short-sleeved T-shirt shows off his biceps. Down in the street, two men in shirtsleeves are sitting in plastic chairs.

Sometimes, night follows night: behind drapes held back by sashes, the orange lights of a city glimmer beyond a stretch of black water, the silhouette of an enormous cypress tree partly concealing the lights festooning a crane; then, from a balcony closed in by a black wrought-iron guardrail, you see the rocky faces of a gorge lined with cascading springs, and the eye follows a winding road dotted with streetlights; then, all the way at the top, you see a dark blue sky, that most-blue blue they call "midnight blue"; and at a window just a few steps over, an immense urban landscape by night comes into view when you pull open the green-and-ochre striped drapes, and then others with a green on beige pattern: a highway glittering with headlights and the rails of a train line divide this view into two, while far in the background, behind a building with a blinking red neon sign for Five Roses Flour, the pale line of a large river cuts the scene horizontally. To the left rises a fifty-story quadrangular tower, and a shorter one shaped like a dihedron, crowned by a sort of glass-clad flying saucer lit from beneath by an intense blue glow. To the right swarms an endless stretch of orange lights, glittering gems, pallid windows. But then, with no transition, next there's suddenly a burst of sunlight on a snowy slope with rocky outcroppings, showing traces of footsteps and snowmobiles, a few telephone poles, with a blue sky overhead. One window over, it's still a winter landscape, but quite different now: passersby all bundled up against the cold waddling among the little brick or sheet metal buildings, and brown and green colored shacks, all lined up beneath an enormous gas storage tank, the whole landscape traversed by wooden telephone poles and power lines, tall industrial chimneys with their plumes of smoke; to the right, behind a building in shiny metal, you can see an oily tanker truck and a cargo plane loading up. You get the feeling this is probably in Russia somewhere, a conjecture borne out by the next window: aerial pipelines wrapped in rags, probably leaking, form a portico above a muddy road strewn with old Ladas that winds among buildings that could be either unfinished or in ruins, it's hard to tell, with yellow, stubbly grass, burnt by the winter, where residual snow patches remain, extending all the way to a birch forest. But here's the next window, whose panels of little leaded panes are set in a deep embrasure, overlooking what could only be Rome: on the left, one recognizes the Church of the Trinitá dei Monti seen almost exactly from the angle Corot must have painted it, then the Quirinal Hill, Nation's Alter, the domes, the cupolas, the Gianicolo behind trees where the setting sun glows red, between a dome that might be Santi Angrogio e Carlo al Corso and Saint Peter's; then, on the right, the heights of Monte Mario behind the cupolas of the twin churches of the Piazza del Pópolo. A swirl of ochres and pinks, as the city lights begin to twinkle on.

At the Belleviews Hotel, eclecticism is pushed to such lengths that not one of the windows that open onto this kaleidoscopic world resembles any other. The disparate nature of the outdoors here matches that of the windows themselves. One consists of three large panes set in a metallic frame painted in cream (through which one can see, to the right, a little parking lot with a palm tree, and, just opposite, a building with opaque windows, none of them lit except the one taped over with bomb-proof adhesive strips, behind which a dimly lit room comes vaguely into view). Dark blue drapes printed in a stylized, pale green and orange floral and fruit pattern, rather pretty (rare enough to merit mention) close over sheer white curtains. Another has no panes at all: it's a darkly lacquered wooden door, almost black, framed in Doric pilasters. It opens, above the rooftops of some Asian city, onto a tiled balcony whose garnet-colored guardrail is set hazardously low. Behind two white vinyl casements trimmed with white lace, wooden shutters mask a scraggy landscape: the rain-soaked red awning of a bistro, a blue and white neon sign flashing "Hotel Restaurant," a streetlamp and chrysanthemum planter pissed on by dogs. Now, that's France! Deep inside two embrasures closed off by pinkish rubberized curtains, a pair of windows, two casements made out of what could be oak—each with two panes hung with little lace curtains showing a pattern of foliage and butterflies—open onto a nearby house, where, on the ground floor, the plate glass window of a restaurant, "The Seagulls," glows in the darkness. A half-rotunda curves around, with two double casement windows, three panes each, through which is visible a palace, banners flying, on the shore of a mountain lake. On the inside, English-style curtains, birds and flowers over blue-green-pink stripes against a beige background, while outside, hunter green shutters slide on separable rails.

Mélanie Melbourne and I never tire of throwing open curtains, pushing out shutters, leaning over balconies, making bets as to what kind of landscape the next window will reveal. Since they're each at different, uneven heights, with gangways leading to each rise and fall, one could almost believe (Mélanie likes to believe) we're perched on a ship's masts, darting about like deckhands. We open the heavy beige fabric drapes, we open the sheer curtains, and there we see, shining under the spongy drizzle, the blacktop of an alleyway with the dark foliage of what might be lilac bushes on either side; some pink hydrangeas are in bloom at the foot of a brick house. In the center of the view, a skein of cables attached to a wooden telephone pole, now listing to one side, cut stripes across the gray sky. Behind some scruffy-looking apartment buildings, the screened-in cage of a driving range (reminiscent of a giant chicken coop) suggests that this must be Japan. Something strangely malefic seems to emanate from this landscape. I don't know what it is, but nothing good could come from that alley, no way, says Mélanie, hugging me tighter. Let's hurry on to another window. It's as if a bit of night has crept in, crept into this room. We open two casements made of cream-colored vinyl behind whitish sheer curtains, not the cleanest. They fly open as the wind and rain burst in. Under the plane trees along a dark street, at the end of which one can make out the Babylonian gate of an enormous edifice covered in green tiles, a slim silhouette in a pink plastic wrap is running away. A bright pink thing where raindrops glisten. But . . . hold on, that's me, she says. Does that mean that I'll be leaving you? But why? Holding hands, we stare at each other, brimming with emotion, and see all that will age us without the other. Parting the macramé curtains and drapes in a purple woolen fabric you could imagine as a Roman emperor's mantle, we lean out of still another window: on the far side of a public square that must be the largest in the world, where police vehicles cast whirling blue lights, there is a gigantic palace, part Stalin, part Venice, spiked with dark pinnacles against the moonlight. Far in the distance, lights twinkle on a peninsula, while to the right a city stretches beneath a soup of clouds, and to the left, beyond a promenade where pathetic little merry-go-rounds turn, two very long jetties thrust into a milky sea. It's then that I recall a line from a Cavafy poem, regarding the death of Mark Antony, which I recited to Mélanie many years ago, when we were staying at the Cecil Hotel: "As one prepared long since, courageously / Say farewell to her, to Alexandria who is leaving": αποχαιρετα την, την Αλεξανδρεια που φευγει.

> *Text handwritten on pages torn out of* Through the Looking Glass, *by Lewis Carroll, Penguin Books.*

37

Room 503, Hotel Dardanija, Radiceva 19, Sarajevo:

Of all the rooms I've stayed in, this is definitely the most complicated to describe. A T-shaped layout, the right angle (inside which the bathroom is located) is slightly truncated. The walls are hung in a kind of pale mauve rayon, with the floor carpeted in a color somewhere in the range between brown and purple. The ceiling, about 2.8 meters high, is polystyrene stamped with geometric shapes—squares and quarter circles—edged in white plastic molding, with a frosted glass ceiling light alongside a fire sprinkler.

To the left of the front door, which is made of varnished wood and has a brass knob, under the cream-colored plastic heating/air-conditioning vent—Gorenje brand—hangs a rectangular mirror in a fluted pale wood frame. Beneath the mirror, a chair made of gold metal tubing holding a round cushion in camouflage colors. Along this wall is a single bed, covered with a shiny, tea-rose pink rayon bedspread, supported by fluted, quadrangular feet, and topped by a headboard in the shape of a pediment (this Parthenon look recurs in all the furnishings).

After that, the wall forms a slightly obtuse angle, which a gradual redressing along its path eventually straightens out. Along this wall, there is first of all a conch-shaped sconce in striated frosted glass with a little pull chain. Beneath the wall lamp, a little table with neo-Grecian fluted columns framing panels of mottled wood holds a Bosch telephone—a model I've never seen before: the idea seems to be that you can set the receiver down any way you want, on a circular support. Next, the wall curves in slightly, so that the second neo-Grecian bed—a perfect replica of the first one described—is separated from it. At the foot of the bed, a hideous painting, in a pale wood frame, represents what looks like a mountain waterfall, trees and snowy peaks in vaporous tones of blue, pink, and rust. At the head of the bed, another "half-shell" sconce.

The wall against which the headboard is placed (though not flush against it, as I've said, since there isn't a real right angle in this whole place) is somewhat complicated to describe. Sorry. Along the bottom, a large white enameled iron radiator. Above it a large bay window made up of four inclined panes, like those in a greenhouse, screened by pink rayon drapes (over sets of Venetian blinds) running along a gold metal curtain rod, forming a kind of canopy or baldachin. Out this window, you can see an S-shaped street: below and to the left is the Bonno pizzeria-café-bar, a clutter of apartment buildings (some in rather poor condition), tile roofs, trees—poplar and birch mostly; and further on, mountains encroached upon by little tile-roofed houses, some of the peaks (left and center) covered in evergreen forests, where low-passing clouds snag and disperse. On the right, the dome of some prestigious building that I can't quite identify (Fine Arts Institute?) rises above the rooftops. This landscape gives off an impression of great sadness (heightened by the white patches that are scattered tombstones).

Inside the T-shape, against the first wall, are arranged a little neo-Grecian cabinet paneled in mottled wood, holding an LG-brand TV; then a table, also neo-Grecian, with a gilt candleholder and red candle. Then, in the beveled part of the angle, the bathroom door in varnished wood. Next, in the recessed part of the wall where the front door is located, the closet nestles: molded pale wood and mottled paneling.

I have no idea whether the strangely skewed configuration of this room, not to mention its postmodern ugliness, has anything to do with the nightmare I've been having (I'm sleeping in the neo-Grecian bed nearest the window). In a city that appears to be Sarajevo (there are minarets, Turkish houses with *mashrabiyas* among Viennese apartment buildings), at some indefinite time (horse-drawn coaches are being driven through the streets, but also army tanks), I'm stalking Medusa. The Lipovan killer seems to span several eras himself (he conceals his hideous flat head under a cap that, like his waxed moustache, brings to mind fin-de-siècle cyclists. His T-shirt, on the other hand, is decidedly modern: black with KILL! spelled out in bright red.). I'm not quite sure why I'm tracking him, but I do know that he has to be prevented from assassinating somebody, at any cost. They were emphatic about that: "At any cost. I'm assuming you understand what that means?" they asked me, at the Train Bleu, where we were having dinner before my departure. That question . . . But who does he want to kill, that's what isn't clear. An architect? An archbishop? Something like that. There are dense throngs of people in the neighborhood of Bascarsija (if indeed the town in question is Sarajevo)—I'm constantly bumping into porters, kebab vendors, a dervish, a shoeshine boy, a soldier, a dancing bear, a pope, a courtesan . . . and wouldn't you know it, near a mosque, my gaze alights on a pair of dark eyes in the slit of a *hijab* that remind me of . . . that can only belong to Pashmina Pachelbel. I come to a halt, think for a moment about stopping her, but then, she's a veiled woman, you can't just grab her arm . . . She's already disappeared, and my brief hesitation was enough for me to lose Medusa's trail as well. I push my way through the crowd, pumping my arms, stepping on slippers, sandals, boots, babouches, and loafers, stammering apologies, fielding insults in several languages, a mustachioed man in a fez spits at my feet, I pay it no mind, I have to catch up with Medusa, but the faster I move, the more I feel I'm bogged down in wet cement. I'm sweating copiously. Finally I spot his cap, way out ahead of me. I plunge into the crowd, bent at the waist, like someone pushing upstream against rapids. When I get to the corner of a bridge . . . (the bridge on which I, myself, killed a priest, in Budapest? But the water below's not nearly wide enough to be the Danube.). Too late! Smoke curls from the barrel of Medusa's revolver, and his target—architect, archaeologist?—he has a strange feathered hat, which rolls along the ground—falls back onto the blood-stained cushions of his carriage. After that, everything becomes even more confused. The consequences seem enormous, dreadful. All of a sudden, I'm buried beneath dead bodies, suffocating under the weight of so many corpses, chilled by coldness of death. I wake up. The room is freezing. I get up to go fiddle with the radiator under the bay window. The heater is broken. The new snow on the mountains shines beneath the moon.

Text handwritten on pages torn out of the Lonely Planet Guide to Africa.[1]

---

1   Madame Anne Laurenceau enlists this unconventional writing paper to support her thesis ("An Archetypal Case of Genre Migration," in *Proceedings from the Third Meeting of Textual Genetics, at the University of Ulan Bator,* vol. 2). According to her, the texts of this book . . . (which we had not yet collected) represent a unique example of a travel guide transformed into, first, a memoir, then an anti-memoir, and finally into a novel; or, rather, the first stages of that process, which she boldly compares, in a flight of lyricism rarely witnessed at university conferences, to the formation of galaxies after the Big Bang. "What we are seeing here is tantamount to the birth of a novel," she writes. "Just as powerful telescopes are getting closer and closer to revealing the state of the universe at its origin, allowing us to reconstitute the stages of evolution and differentiation of cosmic matter, this extraordinary document allows us to witness the transformation of a bit of informational writing—a piece of anti-fiction, if you will—into a work of auto-fiction, and finally into fiction itself." Put more plainly, the author of *Hotel Crystal* is believed to have started out writing a travel guide to hotel rooms worldwide, to which he later added autobiographical details, before heading off into pure fiction. It's a clever hypothesis. Let us simply state that the intent Madame Laurenceau ascribes to our author is about as absurd as the one Borges gives to his character, the emphatic Carlos Argentino Daneri, in "The Aleph"—not very flattering—and that the fact that this text, to which we have assigned the number 37, was written on pages taken from a *Lonely Planet* guidebook ought not to be taken as bringing further evidence to bear on a theory that's rather . . . baroque. *(EN)*

38

Room 217, Granville Island Hotel, 1253 Johnston Street, Granville Island, Vancouver:

The front door, painted a beige-ish mauve and equipped with a Blount, a peephole, and a brass door handle, opens into a hall of about 3 x 1 meters. The walls are hung in a beige imitation fabric, the carpet is coffee-and-cream with coffee-colored squiggles, the ceiling, about 3 meters high, done in white roughcast, has a recessed spotlight. Some heavy white molding runs the length of the junction between the ceiling and the walls. The bathroom door, much like the front door but with a full-length mirror and missing the Blount and the peephole, opens on the right-hand side of the hall, while on the left-hand side there's a little piece of unsigned artwork representing a frozen lake, a pine forest, and some snowy mountains, all in misty tones of bluish-gray and light mauve.

The left-hand wall extends into the room, which measures about 5 x 6 meters. Along this wall, there's a straight-legged table in dark wood with a protective glass top, holding a lamp (two fluted gold metallic columns topped by a beige fabric shade), an ivory telephone, and a coffeemaker and accoutrements; over the table hangs a mirror in a dark wood frame measuring about a meter high by half a meter wide. There's a chair at the table whose seat is upholstered in a blue-green fabric printed in little palm trees. Up against the wall is a rather ugly cabinet made of dark wood with framing around the doors and drawers in red wood. The two upper cabinet doors, with little gold knobs, conceal a minibar (copiously supplied) and a Philips television. Below this are three gold-handled drawers for shirts. Next is a floor lamp with a fluted gold metallic stem and a beige shade, then an armchair upholstered in the same material as the desk chair.

This armchair is located in the corner of the wall facing the front door, which has two plate glass windows, about 1.5 meters wide and 2 meters high, each divided into two panels in metallic frames, the upper one fixed and the lower one with a tilt adjuster. Both windows are shaded by blinds made of large purple slats that can open and close like shutters. Down below, you can see a paved delivery area where a white laundry truck is parked, and beyond, a bench and three newspaper boxes, a grassy knoll above with the tops of a few buildings peeking over. Autumn trees painted cadmium yellow, golden leaves in rain puddles, gray sky. To the left, the boats at the Alder Bay marina.

Abutting the third wall is the bed, enormous (about 2 x 2 meters), covered by a quilted striped bedspread, copper green against brown. The dark wood headboard is flanked by two tall pinnacles in the shape of bowling pins. On either side, little nightstands in two-tone wood, each with a drawer and two doors with gold handles, and a lamp in metallic gold with a truncated beige fabric shade. The table on the left has a Sony radio alarm clock, the right-hand one has an ivory telephone.

The closet, which has an accordion door, is in the fourth wall (behind which is the bathroom). A little painting is hung on it too, by the same artist as the one in the hallway: forests and lake, or a misty inlet. It's entitled *Evening*. It might depict Burrard Inlet in Dollarton, the place where good old Malcolm Lowry lived from 1940 to 1954, where he rewrote *Under the Volcano* five or six times—the first draft of which, long gone, was composed in 1936–37 in Cuernavaca. Well, as it turns out, that draft isn't as long gone as we thought. It's to see this place, which Malcolm calls "Eridanus" in his books, that I've come to Vancouver. To get there, you have to take the Dollarton Highway exit from Second Narrows Ironworkers Memorial Bridge, then keep going until Cates Park, at the entrance to Indian Arm. The wooden house on the shore where he once lived was destroyed a while ago now, but its approximate location is marked by a plaque bolted to a rock: "MALCOLM LOWRY / 1901–1957 / MALCOLM LOWRY, AUTHOR, LIVED / WITH HIS WIFE MARGERIE IN A / SQUATTER'S SHACK NEAR THIS SITE / FROM 1940–1954. HIS WRITINGS HAVE / WON THE GOVERNOR GENERAL'S / AWARD FOR FICTION AND HIS NOVEL / *UNDER THE VOLCANO* / IS OFT DECLARED ONE OF THE FEW / GREAT NOVELS OF THIS CENTURY."[1] Cargo ships move slowly up the sound, the panting of their motors resounding under the soaring trees—red and golden maples, black pines that snag passing clouds. Downstream is a little refinery.

A few days after making this pilgrimage, I was strolling along Hastings Street, on the wrong side of the tracks. I don't know

---

1   The author sketched the rectangle of the plaque and terracing of the lines of text within, perhaps as a tribute to the wish expressed by the author of *Volcano* that the inscriptions sprinkled throughout his novel appear in the typographical format of placards (especially the famous one—for Lowry fans—

¿LE GUSTA ESTE JARDIN?
¿QUE ES SUYO?
¡EVITE QUE SUS HIJOS LO DESTRUYAN!

—with its superfluous question marks). *(EN)*

what induced me to enter a rather pathetic little junk shop—nothing other than idleness, a vague curiosity, the melancholy feeling one often gets in such places that, through the objects on display there (hand-cranked coffee grinders, record players, vinyl records, manual typewriters, wind-up alarm clocks, etc.), one's own youth is up for sale. I was drawn to a rather attractive expandable accordion briefcase, made of rawhide; the clasp still worked, though one of the straps was cut; the fabric that lined the inside was stained and dusty; I got it for twenty Canadian dollars. Back at the hotel, I cautiously began removing part of the old lining, with the idea of having it replaced. I'm sure you've guessed what happened next: the case's interior, underneath the lining, was reinforced with sheets of paper glued right to the leather—some typed, others scrawled in script. I immediately recognized old Malc's handwriting. It wasn't a continuous text (even taking into account that the sheets were probably not placed in any particular order), but various notes (mostly bits of conversation overheard in a cantina, portraits of *borrachos*, some basic lexical items,[2] some observations on the flight of vultures, on a mangy dog, a wounded horse, a rabbit gnawing on a corncob . . .) interspersed with pages where a kind of story was taking shape, not yet hewn from the rough block of words. The notes were handwritten in a script that bouts of drunkenness rendered practically illegible, on all kinds of paper (one in par-

---

2   *Espíon = spy, oso = a bear, absolumente necesario, Box! emocionante peleas,* etc.[3] *(AN)*

3   "*Espíon = spy* (sic = in Spanish *espia* is in fact the word for 'spy'), *oso = a bear absolutely necessary, Boxing! sensational sparring!*" These words or word groups are all found in the definitive version of *Volcano. (EN)*

ticular—wonder of wonders!—on a menu from the El Farolito cantina), and the ink, splattered in places by droplets (of sweat? mescal? rain?) having fallen on the paper, made patterns in places like the silhouettes of trees or a network of nerves. The bits of narrative were typed. Something about a certain Erikson and his wife Priscilla: characters recognizable as primitive versions of the Consul and Yvonne. The briefcase that fate (if not fate, then what?) had put on my path, in a Hastings Street warehouse, was thus papered with scraps of the first manuscript, the lost draft, of *Under the Volcano*! Written in Cuernavaca—the Quauhnahuac of the novel—in 1936-37, at a time when Lowry, who was practically never sober (but "not an hour, not a moment of my drunkenness, my continual death, was not worth it: there is no dross of even the worst of those hours, not a drop of mescal that I have not turned into pure gold, not a drink I have not made sing."[4]) was still living with Jan Gabrial!

I was quick to realize that it would be impossible to remove the sheets of paper without destroying them. But then, the idea of carrying around with me, unbeknownst to anyone by myself, the first draft (or at least the first pages) of one of the books that had meant the most to me, was a very appealing one. Don't the fans of *Under the Volcano* form, in the words of Maurice Nadeau,[5] his French editor, "a strange brotherhood," a kind of

---

4   I'm quoting from memory from Lowry's *Dark as the Grave Wherein My Friend is Laid. (AN)*

5   In a preface which, for many, was one of the first voices beckoning them to literature (and which also contained a few sketchy accounts, as it happens, of the history of the *Volcano* manuscripts). *(AN)*

secret society? So I took the briefcase to a Chinese tailor on Knight Road (he had been one of my associates—or rather, one of my covers—in the SIREN[6] affair), and asked him to fashion a white silk lining. And ever since, this is how I have come to pack shirts, trousers, underwear, and socks between the pages of the first draft of a masterpiece—this is how I have come to use as my overnight bag a treasure that would be the pride of the world's greatest libraries. Someday soon, I'll have to set it down in the Hotel-Casino de la Selva.[7]

> *Text handwritten on pages torn out of* The Life of Joseph Roulin, *by Pierre Michon, Verdier.*

---

6   See "The Full Stop Hotel." *(EN)*

7   This, of course, is the hotel on whose terrace Dr. Vigil and Jacques Laruelle, dressed in white flannel, drink *anís* on the Day of the Dead, in November 1939, right at the opening of *Volcano*. It would appear that the author's plan to travel there was never realized—which might come as a surprise, given how special a place the "Drunken Divine Comedy" held in his imaginings. As for the famous "expandable accordion briefcase," it is, of course, quite tempting to take it for the one Madame *** discovered at Rue des Morillons. Alas, that would be all too easy . . . The case found at Rue des Morillons is indeed made from rawhide, accordion-style. One of its straps has clearly been repaired. It is lined inside with a white fabric that is not silk, but flannel (same as the suits worn by Dr. Vigil and Jacques Laruelle?). But there is no manuscript concealed under this lining, no trace of old glue is discernable. We might add that Madame ***, though she had seen him carrying this case on many occasions during their trips together, has no recollection of his ever alluding to the bibliophile's treasure that might be concealed within—which is hard to explain away using the author's "secret society" allusion, after Maurice Nadeau. On that basis, several open-ended hypotheses become available to us: 1) The briefcase purchased on Hastings Street is not the one fortuitously come upon at Rue des Morillons; 2) It is in fact the same briefcase, but the sheets of paper have been detached without leaving a trace (an art restoration expert at the Louvre has assured us that such an operation is technically possible); 3) It is the same briefcase, and the story told above is a fiction; 4) The briefcase found at Rue des Morillons is a decoy, and consequently, the texts it contains are apocryphal; if such were the case—and, as we have said, we do not support this hypothesis—the Vancouver story would figure as the ironic signature of the hoax. *(EN)*

39

Room 366, Grand Hotel, Varnhagenstrasse 37, Düsseldorf:

The front door, in speckled Havana brown wood, opens onto a hallway of about 2.5 x 1 meters, off which opens another door (on the right), also Havana brown and speckled, with a garnet-colored metal handle, this time leading to the bathroom, and (on the left) the two mirrored sliding doors, framed in Havana wood, of the closet.

The room's ceiling is about 2.5 meters high, painted white. The walls are papered in a white imitation canvas. The carpet is beige, low pile. Along the left-hand wall as you enter is a long cabinet, the same speckled brown wood as the doors, with a minibar built into the left-hand side. The lines of this piece of furniture, which holds, on the left, a pink porcelain lamp with a white shade, and on the right, a Loewe brand TV, are clean, simple and quite elegant. Before you reach the chair, made of pale wood, also well-designed, with the back and seat upholstered in a very pale mauve with a stylized tree print, there's a rectangular mirror measuring about 60 x 30 centimeters, in a pale wood frame, hanging on the wall. Next is a little armchair made of the same pale wood, upholstered in the same fabric as the other chair, and a three-legged console table with a little pink porcelain lamp and white shade. On the wall above, framed in white, a forgettable little painting representing blue flowers, probably forget-me-nots.

The central part of the back wall is occupied by the two large windowpanes, separated by a large mount: each one, framed in white enameled metal and double-paned, measures about 2 meters high by 70 meters wide. Through them you can see, past a low, unlit space (a parking lot, and further on, what are probably courtyards), a row of small apartment buildings and houses whose roofs cut black silhouettes against the dark blue sky. Lights on in their windows. A tall steeple looms over it all, with a building to the right, crowned with red lights, and a factory smokestack, and to the left the tip of a television tower, on the banks of the Rhine, a techno minaret surrounded by a blue glow and more blinking red lights. White sheer curtains run along the length of the wall, as well as plasticized canvas drapes in pale salmon. To the left of the window, a metal radiator lacquered white.

Twin beds are set at a perpendicular angle to the third wall. The bed frames are upholstered in the same pale mauve arboreal pattern described earlier. White comforters, folded in half, lie on each. The headboard and night tables (one between the two beds, with the same lamp as the one on the console, and the other, to the right, with a telephone) are of the same make as the other pieces of furniture: Havana brown burr with rounded edges in blond wood. Above the center night table, a picture of white dahlias against a blue background, suitable but sappy, titled *Dahl 84.* The fourth wall (which abuts the bathroom) is completely bare.

The phone rings: "Dahlia and Forget-Me-Not will be downstairs in five minutes," announces Arak-Bar. Dahlia and Forget-Me-Not are code names that we—Crook, Arak-Bar and myself—have given to the terrible twins. Thick-jawed and heavily mustachioed, they are the favorite sons of a certain Middle-Eastern dictator. Here, they make the rounds of the bars and bordellos, and drag-race through the streets of Düsseldorf in the BMW roadsters they've just bought, one red and one black; miraculously, they haven't run over anyone yet. It's hard to talk about anything serious with these two. They make you wish you could hold them both under a cold shower to straighten them out, but it's probably better not to annoy them. And yet, that's why they're here: to talk seriously. Serious, urgent, and depressing talk. Their daddy has been accused of possessing WMDs, weapons of mass destruction, and he doesn't even have any. He used to, but he doesn't anymore. He sold them all. This is embarrassing for the whole family. How are they going to look now? Like a bunch of fraud, discount dictators, Third World showboats. They would at least like to live up to their reputation as public enemies. And that's where Crook's genius comes in. I'll give you a rough summary of the discussions that took place in the sitting room of this low-profile hotel, in an outlying neighborhood, near the university. To get real WMDs, he explained to them, well, it's too late now, as luck would have it. They should have thought of that before, instead of wasting time torturing their rivals and hanging out with whores in Dubai. But they could at least get some fake bombs, some look-alikes. Then everybody would be happy. President Push is going to go to war against them, that much is certain. And he'll win, it's a foregone conclusion (their four eyes open wide). What's at stake here isn't winning or losing, but honor. Not just theirs, but that of the Arab people (they nod in approval, frown, take on a frightful air). And yet (pay close attention, he tells them: they knit their bull-like brows), and yet, to a certain extent, their interest is the same as President Push's (here, Arak-Bar, in charge of translation, has them repeat this back). Yes, Crook explains: Push, who is using the WMD issue as an excuse for war, knows full well they don't have any (they seem crestfallen). Once he's won, he'll be needing a justification, he'll have to find something, anything that looks at least a little like the much-hyped WMDs: for him, it's also a question of honor (at this point, Dahlia and Forget-Me-Not look completely lost. Crook presses on nevertheless.) So, let's say they get their hands on some junk that amateurish journalists or crooked ones (both are available) can pass off, when the time comes, as weapons of mass destruction, or a lab that's developing them, anyway, everybody's happy, the family honor has been saved, and so has the President's. We don't give a shit about that, retorts Forget-Me-Not haughtily. That's right, we don't give a shit about him, Crook explains patiently, but we still need him: if we want to get him to pass off junk for the real McCoy, his reputation has to be at stake. (One of the things I've learned from spending time with Crook is that the main strength of a conman lies in his patience—though it's also true that you don't always have to deal with guys as thick as Dahlia and Forget-Me-Not: fortunately, there are still some clever suckers out there, who hastily throw themselves into the lion's jaws, who anticipate how a con will work, who even add some new features that we hadn't thought of in our own haste to attain our objective.) Crook reformulates his argument now, taking a different tack.

Anyway—the phone rings: Dahlia and Forget-Me-Not will be downstairs in five minutes. We've nearly convinced them to purchase, cash in hand, five complete brewery installations, totally operational. With their special stainless steel vats, their digital pressure gauges, their pressurized autoclaves, their miles of nickel-plated tubing, they couldn't look more like chemical arms factories. The deal promises to be staggeringly lucrative, as we stand to pocket a triple commission: from the German manufacturer, of course, but also from the CIA who, thanks to us, is looking to set up the "proof" it needs, and even from the Budweiser company, which later on will be able to use this brand-new equipment to produce the millions of gallons of beer required to quench the thirst of the American occupation troops. The deal's in the bag, rejoices Iskandar, we're going to be rolling in it. Be careful, warns Crook, a man of experience: with those two, you can never be sure of anything. Until the last moment . . . And look who's just arriving now. A little tipsy, it seems. This is going to be a contest. They scratch their unshaved chins. They look like *Tintin* characters: Thomson and Thompson dressed up as General Alcazar. Forget-Me-Not speaks up, vociferous. Arak-Bar translates, looking crestfallen. Our friend tells us that honor is all well and good, and certainly has its importance, but what they really want to know is whether the equipment can *also* win the war. Let's not get upset, says Crook, the very picture of tranquility: let's just start again from the beginning.

> *Text handwritten on five pages torn from a notebook, format 11 x 21 centimeters.*

40

Room 205, Grand-Hotel des Balcons, 3 Rue Casimir-Delavigne, Paris 75006:

I'm sure that there are some who will claim that the adventures I'm setting down here (without any embellishment at all—if anything, I'm oversimplifying) are a product of my imagination. This is unavoidable. An inveterate couch potato has a hard time believing that there's such a thing as mountain-climbing. All I can say to those skeptics out there is this: you'll find witnesses to corroborate these stories if you try—some in good faith, others not, but the stories themselves will always remain protected by the ambiguity characteristic of past things, and nothing can prevent that. As for the rooms I described, on the other hand, there's every reason to believe that most of them are still there. So go ahead and check out one or two, or all of them, for that matter, and see if I lied about even ONE detail, however tiny. You'll have no choice but to concede that EVERYTHING is just as I described: carpet patterns and colors, wallpaper, bedspreads, curtains, styles and material of furniture and lamps, landscapes as seen from windows, and the design of those windows, etc. I didn't make up ANY of it (the measurements are approximate, since I had to guess at those, but even then, I always included an adverb such as "about" or "approximately"). So? So, I can already hear the further objection: Going to Hanoi to check whether room 402 of the Dan Chu Hotel actually looks the way I said it did—that's not exactly within most people's means. Granted. In that case, here's one that will cost nothing but a metro ticket for Parisian readers.

It measures about 5 x 5 meters. The door, dark wood, opens directly into the room. The blue carpet is sprinkled with large red and black dots, the walls are done in a synthetic white braid pattern, the ceiling, white, is about 2.5 meters high. The wall on the right as you enter has a radiator consisting of five flat elements that go all the way to the ceiling. A three-pegged coat rack hangs on the wall. Next, there's a luggage rack in dark wood, then a desk with two cupboards made of the same wood on the left. A large mirror (about 2 x 1 meters) in a dark wood frame is affixed to the wall above the desk. On the table top is an Art Nouveau-style lamp—a corolla of petals in frosted glass on a sinuous gold stem—a Barphone brand telephone, and a little Philips television. The floral lamp is twice reflected in my eye, itself reflected in the mirror: once, clearly (the tulip-like shape is distinguishable) in my green iris specked with glowing ochre (a kind of moldy Mars), and a second time, smaller, on the border of my dark pupil. I recall something I read recently in a book by the painter Cueco, something indisputably factual, but which I'd never noticed before until now: no one, ever, has seen his own eyes, except in a reflection. In front of the desk, a chair with leather upholstery on the back and seat.

The wall facing the door has a window measuring about 2 x 1 meters, composed of two white PVC casements with single panes, behind a set of net curtains and spinach-colored drapes.

White metallic shutters are opened on either side of a tiny balcony with a black wrought iron guardrail. To the left, you can see the Odéon Theater under renovation, wrapped in tarpaulins billowing in the wind like sails. Theater on the high seas. Directly opposite there's a five-story building, not counting the mansards, its façade recently repainted in a cream color; at a window situated at the same height as mine, an Asian man sits at his computer, under an architect's lamp. At street level, shops: the La Cambuse restaurant, AGR Real Estate, Sorbonne Printing and Repro, MacDougall. An orange streetlight is riveted to the façade above and to the left of "The Chinaman." To the right, at the end of Casimir-Delavigne, is Rue Monsieur-le-Prince and the staircase of a street whose name I forget (Antoine Dubois?), which leads down to the Medical School. A shop selling anatomical models and plates is on the corner. Directly below my window, a little awning protects the hotel entrance, which is next-door to a strangely (and sadly) poetic sign that reads: "The House of Orphaned Diseases," a quaint term in French which simply means, "rare."

The twin beds, covered in a raspberry fabric, abut the third wall, their dark wood headboards each bearing a floral Art Nouveau sconce. Above each is a framed poster for an art exhibit: on the right, a young woman in a long red dress and black hat, riding crop in hand, extends an invitation to "Reynolds at the Grand Palais, 9 October through 16 December 1985"; on the left, a portrait of Erasmus at work advertises "the paintings of Hans Holbein the Younger at the Louvre, 18 January through

15 April 1985." After that, the wall forms a right angle to enclose the bathroom.

Henri Michaux, the man of a thousand hotels, lived here in 1931-32; it was here that he wrote *A Barbarian in Asia*. Knowing this, and also knowing that the so-called "Chinaman" across the way is in fact Japanese, and, more precisely, the cardiologist of the Great Leader of the Rpop#%µ©!!¾œ□2&,[1] whose systolic patterns he is scrutinizing on his computer screen, and that Rue Monsieur-le-Prince is full of shadowy Chinese storefronts (supposedly) peddling material for acupuncture, for "moxibustion," facial and foot reflexology, pendulums, sex manuals . . . [2]

. . . with SIREN.[3] Officially, my contact was a clothing store up the Rue de l'Odéon, a female contact, as it happens, a very silky Chinese woman (that's another story, which I might tell someday, though I can't be sure), but in truth . . . [4]

. . . spell it out for you? The building opposite was freshly painted. You don't . . . [5]

---

1   Crossed out, illegible—cf. note 2 of "room" 34. *(EN)*

2   A squirt of liquid (it appears to be sea water) has irretrievably erased a dozen lines, leaving behind nothing but a cloud of diluted ink surrounded by streaks. As it stands, there's no denying that the text remains quite mysterious. Our attempts to construe some meaning here have been fruitless. Will someone else's more ingenious attempts prove successful? This is our hope, in any case, and we request that anyone who has managed to make a plausible story out of this gap-ridden text kindly get in touch with us. We've reason to fear, however, that some data indispensable for making sense out of the text has disappeared along with its "laundered" section, making even an approximate restoration practically impossible. *(EN)*

3   Cf. "The Full Stop Hotel." *(EN)*

4   A streak has erased the end of this sentence. *(EN)*

5   Idem. *(EN)*

. . . doesn't sound familiar to you? No? Not even the shop on the corner of Rue Monsieur-le-Prince, or the kind of merchandise they sold? That all goes back to the time Themistocles arrived on the scene in Seattle, to repatriate the corpses of the illegal Chinese immigrants to Shanghai, hidden in crates of . . . [6]

. . . In that case . . . I'm afraid you're clearly not cut out for a life of adventure. But rest assured, you can still be a perfectly good writer without all that. Not all scribblers are spies, don't believe it for a minute, nor are they all alcoholics,[7] no, certainly not. Or professional revolutionaries. Some are, of course, but not all. Those are ideas you only find in books, I assure you. In general, it's a nice, comfortable little life. Not luxurious, no golden parachute, but not dangerous either. Really.

Well, on that note, I'm feeling a bit tired. I'm sorry. I'm going to turn in now. You won't forget to turn off the lights, will you?

> *Text handwritten on pages torn from* The Dictionary of Imaginary Places, *by Alberto Manguel and Gianni Guadalupi, Harcourt.*

---

6   Idem. *(EN)*
7   The author is alluding here to the end of *Under the Volcano. (EN)*

41

Room of Noises, Hotel du Départ:[1]

Have I been drugged, or did I just have too much to drink? As Michaux describes it in his little text entitled "Trying to Wake Up," I feel less like a body stretched out on a bed than "a sea of clouds." It would be inaccurate to say that noises are reaching my ears, since, in this gaseous state, I don't have any ears (or any other organs either, for that matter, nor any anatomical differentiation whatsoever): noises, then, are resounding in the vapor. All kinds of noises, a cacophony. The rumbling of busses shifting gear, horns honking, the basso continuo of traffic, police sirens, etc. A steeple bell strikes three, a muezzin chants a call to prayer. Planes land and take off, the engines are in hysterics. Someone's prodigious snoring shakes the partition wall. Foghorns issue their lugubrious call (and I'm sure, despite my gaseous state, that they are sounding in the port of Alexandria[2]). The bellowing of drunken soldiers can be heard in the corridor, doors slam violently. Oddly enough, these overpowering, despotic noises

---

1   What follows is a scratched out address, illegible. Could it possibly be the hotel at number 19, Rue du Départ, in Paris (two-star, all modern conveniences)? The station mentioned, in that case, would be the Gare de Montparnasse. But the Rue du Départ is not an avenue, nor is it lined with plane trees. Of course, the Hotel Metropole in Metz comes to mind as well (cf. room 18), but this scene of Mélanie Melbourne's departure is quite different. (EN)
2   For it's true that, as Michaux again states in the aforementioned text, one lies in this state "the way you sometimes lie in the bed of a constantly repeated melody without being able to get out of it, no matter how hard you try." (AN)

leave the softer, more discreet ones alone to go about their noisy little business: I notice (which is to say, the thing that will soon call itself "I" notices) a humming that might be coming from the air-conditioner, or a vent of some kind, then a rustling and babbling that seems to be produced by falling water, the gargling of radiators, the bell-like tinkling of halyards against masts, the steady breathing of waves reaching the shore. Somewhere, a dog is barking endlessly.

Progressively (an infinitely slow progression, despite being enclosed within the span of a few minutes, at most), this disharmonious orchestra subsides, fades away. The instruments go silent one after another, with only one still left by the end: the slamming of a door. As all this sound dwindles, as though it were transmuting into solid matter, I leave my gaseous state for a more solid one as well—though still far removed from my normal shape: something like a vaulting horse stuck lying in a bed. But I'm evolving apace, and soon, here I am again, myself. A horrible premonition (but is it really a premonition?) sweeps through me: what if Mélanie Melbourne has left? I reach over. Nothing there, where she should be. I reach again, patting the mattress—nothing. A door slams. I raise myself on one elbow and sit up, jump out of bed. Her cheap little pink plastic raincoat's not on the chair, her suitcase isn't on the rack, her . . . my God, she's really gone! I run to the window and open it, not caring that I'm stark naked. Nothing—rain makes the plane trees glisten, the wind picks up leaves and drops them into the dark puddles along the avenue leading to the train station. From up here, they look like severed hands. An old hag, peeking out from under her umbrella and catching sight of me, lets out a little scream.[3] Somewhere, a dog is barking endlessly.

> *Text handwritten on a blank page from the literary journal* Scherzo, *18-19, a special double issue devoted to Olivier Rolin.*

---

3 Professor Olender has pointed out that this scene reads like a burlesque version of the one from the *Odyssey* (Book VI), where Nausicaa discovers Ulysses. *(EN)*

Room 8, Au Bon Accueil Hotel, 39 Rue Marceau, Saint-Nazaire:

The front door leads right into the room, which is carpeted in beige bouclé. It has a sloping ceiling that follows the line of the roof on the right. The wall where the front door is located is wallpapered in a pinkish beige with geometric patterns. To the right of the door, a full-length mirror, frameless, is affixed to the wall, as are two coat hooks. To the left, under glass, is a list of the hotel's house rules (and as none of them is in any way unreasonable, I'll forego transcribing them here).

The wall on the right is, as I said, sloping. It is papered in a pinkish-beige floral pattern (as is the wall opposite the door). A skylight of about 1 x 1 meters is set into the slope . . . [1]

> *Text handwritten on a page torn from* Pura Vida, *by Patrick Deville, Seuil.*

---

[1]   The description is interrupted here, having barely begun. We can therefore suppose (though this supposition can be in no way conclusive) that this is the last "room" undertaken by the author. It is mentioned, you will note, in the text that we have entitled "The Full Stop Hotel," which would seem to confirm our conjecture that the latter might be not so much a prose poem in the style of Larbaud and Cendrars as a set of notes for the work to follow. We are able to discover, thanks to this text, that the story that would have continued under the heading "Bon Accueil" is the one about Crook's attempt to sell the Saint-Nazaire submarine base to Dahlia and Forget-Me-Not (alias Barabas and Pomdapi). *(EN)*

The Full Stop Hotel:

The Garden Hotel of Surabaya where we were living like kings with Themistocles, back when he was commander of the *Gahaya Komodo* (Komodo Dragon), a schooner that shipped wood from Pontianak and Banjarmasin,

The Grand Palms Hotel, on the Via Roma in Palermo, where Raymond Roussel died, and where I spent an entire night listening to the outrageous snoring of Rhinoceros Man in the adjacent room,

Hotel Hyundai on Semenovskaya Street in Vladivostok, where, undercover as a street photographer, I spied on the Soviet Far East Fleet (and Antonomarenko, hot on my trail, was so fooled by my disguise that he came to the port one day and had me take his picture with a Korean whore),

The Terrace Hotel, on Jalan Tasek Lama Street in Bandar Seri Begawan, where I read Michaux and had three nightmares: one where I fell flat on my ass, another where I was killed by a Finnish Communist, and then a third where Mélanie Melbourne left me (and that one was true),

West End Hotel on New Marine Lines in Mumbai, where I made the acquaintance of a gorgeous Russian woman whose father commanded a ballistic missile base in Sakhalin (as for her, she was dabbling in ruby smuggling),

The Bellevue Syrene Hotel, in Sorrento, where, on the back of an envelope, Jane did a pen drawing of me in a dark bathrobe against the bay of Naples, with Vesuvius as a big sombrero,

The Hotel Le Cedre, on the road to Banyuls, in Port-Vendres, where I saw a giant squid drag a small boat out to sea, from my window in room 1, at dawn, almost right under the jetty on the port,

The Cathedral Hotel in Strasburg, where I spent days doing nothing but watching the tower of the cathedral, which looked like a pink rocket about to take off,

The Hotel Acropole, *shāriaa* Zubeir in Khartoum, which I described under a different name in a novel, (French windows with pale blue shutters opening onto a white-hot terrace overlooking sheet-metal roofs and brick shacks strewn with debris, set around a courtyard where a bougainvillea was growing),

The Port-Sudan Palace where I stayed with Papadiamantides when we were using his dhow to smuggle alcohol over to Sudan, at the risk of a public flogging (out the window we could see an empty lot, one-story ochre buildings with green shutters, a few palm trees, cranes at the port),

The Hotel Eibar, *calle* Florida in Buenos Aires, where the *telefonista*, a dead ringer for Gina Lollobrigida, came up to my room on the ninth floor, and I wasn't up to the task (life isn't always rosy),

Pensacola Grand Hotel, in Florida, in whose magnificent bar—dimly lit, paneled, covered with photographs of Navy pilots and planes—Arlette Harlowe clued me in about the Commander Terry Anderson deal—but that's another story, which I'll tell when the time comes,[1]

---

1   He already has (cf. "room" 12, where Terry Anderson is, incidentally, not a commander but a lieutenant colonel, and therefore, an officer of the Air Force, not the Navy). *(EN)*

Hotel Riviera in Havana, where I fell in love with a dancer at the Tropicana Cabaret, whose motto was *un paraíso bajo las estrellas,* a paradise under the stars,

The Grand Hotel de Sète, which I described in a novel, where Leper-Head Hans served drinks to Leila and me on the patio surrounded by a gangway which (the word) called to mind a ferryboat, or (the thing itself) a prison,

The Perry Hotel in Petoskey, Michigan, where I used to stay whenever I would go trout fishing with Hemingway along the Big Two-Hearted River,

York House, Rua das Janelas Verdes in Lisbon, where I wrote the following poem (if you can call it poetry) one night when I couldn't stand the way I looked:

In hotels, people always write in front of mirrors

Late at night

You watch your beard grow

The circles under your eyes darken.

Nome. O seu nome.

Bare-chested, sweating

Growth of beard

Cigarette glowing red

You look like somebody who should be shot

A head full of glass shards

Head shards waiting to explode

All right, calm down.

Now, I hear

A siren on the Tage

The little bells of the *eléctricos*

The clacking of the jaws

On the Rue des Fenêtres-Vertes

Of trucks devouring trash cans,

The Cleopatra Hotel in Bir Safaga on the Red Sea, where I read the Koran, a bit distracted however by the fact that the receptionist embodied my idea (a pleasant one) of how Cleopatra must have looked,

The Hotel Juong Duong in My Tho, which I depict in a novel, above a tributary of the Mekong, crowded with fishing boats garlanded with red flags,

The Hotel Chari in N'Djamena, where I read Gombrowicz's *Journal*; I recall a black leg beneath a star-studded, midnight-blue dress, and shoes with golden laces, at the Booby, on Bokassa Avenue; I also recall (a more prosaic memory) that when whites got together at mosquito-and-cocktail hour, in a dusty garden that extended down to the river, they always went on about diseases, pulmonary edema, psoriasis, malaria, tapeworm, and various monumental bouts of the runs,

The Hotel Caravelas, on Pico Island in the Azores, where I would go whoring whenever I'd killed a sperm whale, back when I was a harpooner on Gil de Brum Avila's *canoa*,

Youth Hostel #1, above the Bambola snack bar in Piraeus, where I first met Themistocles Papadiamantides, before he had become a seaman, but was still a fish (puzzle worthy of the Sphinx!).

The Hotel des Alpes, Rue des Alpes, in Geneva, near the Cornavin station, where I spent a night behind the curtains of room 102, my left arm supporting my right, armed with a Glock

17 fitted with a silencer (in the famous Agent 007 pose), eyes glued to the neon-lit entrance of the Hotel Montana across the street: though Medusa didn't show that night, having missed his train (still, just wait and see),

Hotel Olümpia in Tallinn, where a ravishing girl was waitress at the snack bar on the fourteenth floor: a helmet of pale blond hair, such pale blue eyes, milky skin, diaphanous in every way, absolutely Nordic, aurora borealis, polar-magnetic,

The Hotel President, on Zamalek Island in Cairo, where I was staying when I made the acquaintance of the third daughter of the third wife of the Imam of Al-Azhar, the divine Leila, absolutely Southern (she was in the habit of sunbathing directly below my window, in moderately Islamic swimwear, in the gardens of the Chinese ambassador, where she was employed),

The Saint George Lycabettus Hotel, on Kleomenous Street, where we landed (and a very pleasant landing it was, on the shoals of Athens) after Themistocles had smuggled us, Leila and I, out of Port Saïd,

The Hotel Villages where, unbeknownst to him, I saw my brother watching, from the window of room 611, the last sunset of the twentieth century stretch its shadow over the Paris beltway, between the Grands Moulins de Pantin and the high-rises that face each other at the corner of Boulevard Ney and Rue de la Chapelle,

The Hotel Yalta in Yalta, Crimea, where I met Iskandar Arak-Bar who was acting as translator for a Ba'ath Party delegation invited to tour the achievements of seaside socialism, but what he was really interested in was Chekhov (and what's so odd is that our friendship, during which we would rarely have water on our table, began in the water, since I saved him from drowning one day when he was dead drunk),

Гостиница Красная, The Red Hotel, on Pushkinskaia in Odessa, where Pavel Schmelk, the ingenious engineer, who spent his holidays there, and who would do crossword puzzles in seven languages (Czech, obviously, Russian, by force of circumstance, Finnish, Hungarian, German, English, and French), came looking for me one day, in the crimson velvet upholstered dining room, to ask if I could help him find an answer to a Eugene Maleska puzzle that was stumping him ("crimson chart-topper," fourteen letters[2]),

The Rex Hotel, above City Hall in Saigon, a carbon copy of l'Hôtel de Ville in Paris, where, using my room as main office, I managed SIREN (Silk International Enterprise), a joint venture devoted officially to exporting shirts and silk pajamas, but, in actual fact, to selling weaponry of all sorts, recovered from the battlefields of Vietnam by generals of the People's Army interested in making deals and in friendship among nations: and all that (believe it or not), I did for the love of an incredibly beautiful girl, an Annamese princess that I'd met when she was selling roasted dogs over by the racetrack,

The Hotel Alexander, on Rue Adib Ishak in Beirut, where a 120 mm rocket shot through my room without exploding while I was asleep,[3]

---

2 *Internationale. (EN)*
3 Though it did wake me up. *(AN)*

The Hotel Au Bon Accueil, Rue Marceau in Saint-Nazaire, where Crook tried to sell a submarine base to Dahlia and Forget-Me-Not: "turnkey contract, carriage paid," he guaranteed (but the twins, though they never managed to figure out exactly what it was, could sense that there was something funny going on),

The Hotel Metropole, Place de Brouckère, in Brussels, where Monsignor Fottorino, disguised as a Milanese businessman, showed up for duty,

The Police Station Hotel, Place Maubert, where I happened to spend a night sobering up on the ceramic tile floor of the drunk tank, stretched out like a corpse in a morgue,

The Inn on Destin Harbor, in Florida, where I decided to stay because it was, well, my destiny, and there she was, in the restaurant, at a table near mine, a pretty blonde who looked bored with her aerodynamic athlete of a husband, and who was giving me the eye, the ideal situation for getting myself punched in the face, but to make a long story short, we did end up making love, very delightfully but cautiously, she and I, in the king-size bed in room 114, right next to her hulking husband, who was completely knocked out from alcohol and sunstroke (the jerk had spent the entire day parasailing), after which we smoked the erstwhile classic cigarette on the balcony, overlooking the jade rectangle of the swimming pool and the jet-black water of the marina, without the least concern for the slumbering parachutist,

Shirakabe-so, in Amagi-Yugashima, a traditional Japanese ryokan, all in dark wood and pearled light, with murmuring water, where I go every so often to relax (in light of all the foregoing, you might be justified in concurring that mine is an exhausting life),

The Hotel du Lion d'Or, in Saint-Chély-d'Apcher, where Perec slept (though he forgot, as he says in *Species of Spaces,* the wallpaper pattern), about which I corresponded with a nurse in the Saint-Alban psychiatric hospital, but where I have never actually stayed, despite my wish to do so,

The Red Roof Inn, on East Ontario in Chicago, where I did nothing special,

The Hotel Crystal, Rue Chanzy in Nancy, about which I still don't remember a thing . . . [4]

> *Text handwritten on four pages torn from* Mémoires d'outre-tombe, *by Chateaubriand, Gallimard, "Quarto" collection.*

4　At this point, mention should probably be made of the ingenious hypothesis—a bit too ingenious, perhaps—proposed by Professor Aptekman, which posits that the collection of these "rooms" is nothing, according to his rather martial metaphor, but "a multi-pronged assault attempting to besiege the dark entity, the unconquered citadel of the past, ironically referred to by a name—Crystal—to be read not as the name of a hotel, of course, but as an oxymoronic black crystal, the heart of darkness, impervious to memory, around which revolves (like stars around a black hole) the work of memory—literature being none other than this act of orbiting around an empty space, this abyss into which it inevitably, finally, plummets. Thus, 'I remember a thousand hotels, not the Hotel Crystal' means only this: 'What happened in my story that I have cast out of my story, and who is making me write it (making me trace the concentric circles of writing), and who is out to get me?' The multiple occurrences of the letter 'y' of the so-called 'address' (Hotel Crystal, rue Chanzy, in Nancy) are there, if I may say, to ask the question 'why here?': in French, 'y' means 'here'—*hic Rhodus, hic salta* (the Latin *hic,* whence comes the French adverb of place 'y,' let us recall). And here, hic, what happens? It is here that we come upon a fork in the road—look at the letter 'y' itself—here that a bifurcation occurs, that the *clinamen* comes about." (In *The Journal of Found Objects,* vol. 54, issue 22). *(EN)*

Index of Proper Names

SELECTED DALKEY ARCHIVE PAPERBACKS

PETROS ABATZOGLOU, *What Does Mrs. Freeman Want?*
PIERRE ALBERT-BIROT, *Grabinoulor.*
YUZ ALESHKOVSKY, *Kangaroo.*
FELIPE ALFAU, *Chromos.*
    Locos.
IVAN ÂNGELO, *The Celebration.*
    The Tower of Glass.
DAVID ANTIN, *Talking.*
ANTÓNIO LOBO ANTUNES, *Knowledge of Hell.*
ALAIN ARIAS-MISSON, *Theatre of Incest.*
DJUNA BARNES, *Ladies Almanack.*
    Ryder.
JOHN BARTH, *LETTERS.*
    Sabbatical.
DONALD BARTHELME, *The King.*
    Paradise.
SVETISLAV BASARA, *Chinese Letter.*
MARK BINELLI, *Sacco and Vanzetti Must Die!*
ANDREI BITOV, *Pushkin House.*
LOUIS PAUL BOON, *Chapel Road.*
    Summer in Termuren.
ROGER BOYLAN, *Killoyle.*
IGNÁCIO DE LOYOLA BRANDÃO, *Teeth under the Sun.*
    Zero.
BONNIE BREMSER, *Troia: Mexican Memoirs.*
CHRISTINE BROOKE-ROSE, *Amalgamemnon.*
BRIGID BROPHY, *In Transit.*
MEREDITH BROSNAN, *Mr. Dynamite.*
GERALD L. BRUNS,
    Modern Poetry and the Idea of Language.
EVGENY BUNIMOVICH AND J. KATES, EDS.,
    Contemporary Russian Poetry: An Anthology.
GABRIELLE BURTON, *Heartbreak Hotel.*
MICHEL BUTOR, *Degrees.*
    Mobile.
    Portrait of the Artist as a Young Ape.
G. CABRERA INFANTE, *Infante's Inferno.*
    Three Trapped Tigers.
JULIETA CAMPOS, *The Fear of Losing Eurydice.*
ANNE CARSON, *Eros the Bittersweet.*
CAMILO JOSÉ CELA, *Christ versus Arizona.*
    The Family of Pascual Duarte.
    The Hive.
LOUIS-FERDINAND CÉLINE, *Castle to Castle.*
    Conversations with Professor Y.
    London Bridge.
    North.
    Rigadoon.
HUGO CHARTERIS, *The Tide Is Right.*
JEROME CHARYN, *The Tar Baby.*
MARC CHOLODENKO, *Mordechai Schamz.*
EMILY HOLMES COLEMAN, *The Shutter of Snow.*
ROBERT COOVER, *A Night at the Movies.*
STANLEY CRAWFORD, *Some Instructions to My Wife.*
ROBERT CREELEY, *Collected Prose.*
RENÉ CREVEL, *Putting My Foot in It.*
RALPH CUSACK, *Cadenza.*
SUSAN DAITCH, *L.C.*
    Storytown.
NICHOLAS DELBANCO, *The Count of Concord.*
NIGEL DENNIS, *Cards of Identity.*
PETER DIMOCK,
    A Short Rhetoric for Leaving the Family.
ARIEL DORFMAN, *Konfidenz.*
COLEMAN DOWELL, *The Houses of Children.*
    Island People.
    Too Much Flesh and Jabez.
RIKKI DUCORNET, *The Complete Butcher's Tales.*
    The Fountains of Neptune.
    The Jade Cabinet.
    Phosphor in Dreamland.
    The Stain.
    The Word "Desire."
WILLIAM EASTLAKE, *The Bamboo Bed.*
    Castle Keep.
    Lyric of the Circle Heart.
JEAN ECHENOZ, *Chopin's Move.*
STANLEY ELKIN, *A Bad Man.*
    Boswell: A Modern Comedy.
    Criers and Kibitzers, Kibitzers and Criers.
    The Dick Gibson Show.
    The Franchiser.
    George Mills.
    The Living End.
    The MacGuffin.
    The Magic Kingdom.
    Mrs. Ted Bliss.
    The Rabbi of Lud.
    Van Gogh's Room at Arles.

ANNIE ERNAUX, *Cleaned Out.*
LAUREN FAIRBANKS, *Muzzle Thyself.*
    Sister Carrie.
LESLIE A. FIEDLER,
    Love and Death in the American Novel.
GUSTAVE FLAUBERT, *Bouvard and Pécuchet.*
FORD MADOX FORD, *The March of Literature.*
JON FOSSE, *Melancholy.*
MAX FRISCH, *I'm Not Stiller.*
    Man in the Holocene.
CARLOS FUENTES, *Christopher Unborn.*
    Distant Relations.
    Terra Nostra.
    Where the Air Is Clear.
JANICE GALLOWAY, *Foreign Parts.*
    The Trick Is to Keep Breathing.
WILLIAM H. GASS, *A Temple of Texts.*
    The Tunnel.
    Willie Masters' Lonesome Wife.
ETIENNE GILSON, *The Arts of the Beautiful.*
    Forms and Substances in the Arts.
C. S. GISCOMBE, *Giscome Road.*
    Here.
DOUGLAS GLOVER, *Bad News of the Heart.*
    The Enamoured Knight.
WITOLD GOMBROWICZ, *A Kind of Testament.*
KAREN ELIZABETH GORDON, *The Red Shoes.*
GEORGI GOSPODINOV, *Natural Novel.*
JUAN GOYTISOLO, *Count Julian.*
    Makbara.
    Marks of Identity.
PATRICK GRAINVILLE, *The Cave of Heaven.*
HENRY GREEN, *Blindness.*
    Concluding.
    Doting.
    Nothing.
JIŘÍ GRUŠA, *The Questionnaire.*
GABRIEL GUDDING, *Rhode Island Notebook.*
JOHN HAWKES, *Whistlejacket.*
AIDAN HIGGINS, *A Bestiary.*
    Bornholm Night-Ferry.
    Flotsam and Jetsam.
    Langrishe, Go Down.
    Scenes from a Receding Past.
    Windy Arbours.
ALDOUS HUXLEY, *Antic Hay.*
    Crome Yellow.
    Point Counter Point.
    Those Barren Leaves.
    Time Must Have a Stop.
MIKHAIL IOSSEL AND JEFF PARKER, EDS., *Amerika:*
    Contemporary Russians View the United States.
GERT JONKE, *Geometric Regional Novel.*
JACQUES JOUET, *Mountain R.*
HUGH KENNER, *The Counterfeiters.*
    Flaubert, Joyce and Beckett:
    The Stoic Comedians.
    Joyce's Voices.
DANILO KIŠ, *Garden, Ashes.*
    A Tomb for Boris Davidovich.
ANITA KONKKA, *A Fool's Paradise.*
GEORGE KONRÁD, *The City Builder.*
TADEUSZ KONWICKI, *A Minor Apocalypse.*
    The Polish Complex.
MENIS KOUMANDAREAS, *Koula.*
ELAINE KRAF, *The Princess of 72nd Street.*
JIM KRUSOE, *Iceland.*
EWA KURYLUK, *Century 21.*
VIOLETTE LEDUC, *La Bâtarde.*
DEBORAH LEVY, *Billy and Girl.*
    Pillow Talk in Europe and Other Places.
JOSÉ LEZAMA LIMA, *Paradiso.*
ROSA LIKSOM, *Dark Paradise.*
OSMAN LINS, *Avalovara.*
    The Queen of the Prisons of Greece.
ALF MAC LOCHLAINN, *The Corpus in the Library.*
    Out of Focus.
RON LOEWINSOHN, *Magnetic Field(s).*
D. KEITH MANO, *Take Five.*
BEN MARCUS, *The Age of Wire and String.*
WALLACE MARKFIELD, *Teitlebaum's Window.*
    To an Early Grave.
DAVID MARKSON, *Reader's Block.*
    Springer's Progress.
    Wittgenstein's Mistress.
CAROLE MASO, *AVA.*
LADISLAV MATEJKA AND KRYSTYNA POMORSKA, EDS.,
    Readings in Russian Poetics: Formalist and
    Structuralist Views.

FOR A FULL LIST OF PUBLICATIONS, VISIT:
www.dalkeyarchive.com

SELECTED DALKEY ARCHIVE PAPERBACKS

FOR A FULL LIST OF PUBLICATIONS, VISIT:
www.dalkeyarchive.com